River Steps Free

Crawdad Beach Series (Book 6)

Lisa Buffaloe

Visit the author's website at https://lisabuffaloe.com.

ISBN: 9781957715315 (eBook)
ISBN: 9781957715322 (Paperback)
ISBN: 9781957715339 (Hardcover)

Cover design by JoAnn Durgin, JoAnn's Book Cover Design

River Steps Free

River Sawyer belonged to no one and nowhere. With those thoughts, she fled the only home she'd ever known in her grandmother's broken-down car. River hoped to make it to the ocean, but the vehicle had other ideas and gave its last shudder on a lonely, deserted road.

When a friendly couple picked her up and drove her to Crawdad Beach, River wasn't sure if she'd entered the twilight zone or paradise. There was no way people could be this kind. Or could they?

Sammie Banks stayed busy working at Doohickeys Hardware Store, taking online college courses, and helping his parents on their farm during his off hours. His life was basically full and satisfying. However, something was missing. Or maybe it was someone.

Book 6 of the Crawdad Beach Series.

Table of Contents

River Steps Free iv

Table of Contents v

Chapter 1 1

Chapter 2 11

Chapter 3 19

Chapter 4 26

Chapter 5 34

Chapter 6 39

Chapter 7 45

Chapter 8 54

Chapter 9 59

Chapter 10 65

Chapter 11 72

Chapter 12 79

Chapter 13 85

Chapter 14 91

Chapter 15 98

Chapter 16 105

Chapter 17 112

Chapter 18 118

Chapter 19 125

Chapter 20 130

Chapter 21 135

Chapter 22 142

Chapter 23 145

Chapter 24 148

Epilogue 153

To the Reader 155

Acknowledgments 157

About the Author 158

Chapter 1

The car will go as far as you need to go.

River Sawyer sighed at the words her grandmother had said when she handed River the car keys. Her sneakers scuffed along the side of the two-lane road as she dragged her bags behind her.

Nana's old vehicle had only gone a thousand miles before it died. Not just stopped, exploded. Not a massive explosion like the action movies, more like a poof of a smoky fireball as the car disintegrated into a metal skeletal charred heap.

And, of course, it happened on a deserted road in the middle of the night where no one would come to help. At least River had been able to rescue her phone, charger, backpack, and suitcases containing her few belongings. With only five hundred dollars in cash and a few hundred on her pay-as-you-go credit card, she needed to find a job soon.

She'd left her hometown seventeen hours ago, stopping for gas, food, and a quick nap. The small Texas town where she'd grown up hadn't been a bad place, but the house where she'd lived was another matter.

River's high school graduation had been a few days ago and she'd planned on staying to ensure her grandmother was cared for, but Nana made River leave and promise to never return. Even her pet tomcat had run off with the hussy feline that used to come calling late at night.

Nana's caretaker, Zachariah, had stayed to watch over her grandmother. But even that knowledge didn't soothe River's pain. Two hours into her trip, Zachariah had called to let her know her grandmother was in a better place. River swallowed a sob. Why hadn't Nana let her stay until she passed? Why did she make River leave? Nana had told her to trust God, that He would take care of her.

River knew her parents wouldn't miss her back in Texas, and she sure wouldn't miss them. She'd never understand why they had adopted her as a baby. There wasn't a time she felt loved or wanted by her parents. River swiped her tears away. Crying about the past didn't change anything.

As the sun rose, a bird sang in the trees. At least someone was in a good mood. River stopped, sat on her larger suitcase, removed her sneakers, and rubbed her tired feet. Maybe she should have taken the freeway instead of continuing on the country road, but she didn't have a smartphone, so she didn't have GPS, and Nana's old map didn't even show a major highway.

At least it wasn't raining, and the temperature was decent. If River could make it to the beach, a hotel or restaurant would hopefully give her a job.

She'd only visited the ocean a few times and didn't sunbathe, but her skin kept a decent tan. She figured someone from her birth heritage must have been Italian or Spanish. With her blue-grey eye color, she never could figure that out.

Whatever she was, she needed to keep going. River said a prayer that God would continue to guide her. She put her shoes back on, got to her feet, and kept walking.

Up ahead, a silver pickup drove toward her. The truck slowed as it got near, drove past, then turned around and stopped behind her.

Cringing, River prayed for protection as she took mace out of her backpack. Readying herself for action, she turned to face whoever stopped.

The side passenger door opened, and an older woman with a bouffant hairdo hurried her way. "Good morning! I'm Maybelline Taylor. Could we give you a lift somewhere?"

River blinked a few times. Should she trust this lady? She did remind her a little of her grandmother.

Maybelline smiled what looked like a sweet smile. "My husband Chester is in the truck. You can trust us." She gave a soft chuckle. "I know that sounds funny to say, but you really can. We felt led to get up early this morning and go for a drive, and here you are."

The driver's side door on the pickup opened, and a silver-haired gentleman stepped out and waved.

"That's my husband, Chester." Maybelline waved back at him.

Okay, too strange. River stood there, unsure what to do, not that she had many options.

"Do you have a car we could get towed for you, or did someone drop you off?" Maybelline asked.

River shook her head. "My car won't need towing." She didn't want to tell the lady more than needed about her situation.

"Okay." Maybelline gave her a curious look and then pointed in the direction River had been heading. "We live in Crawdad Beach and would be happy to drive you there."

"I guess so. I'm hoping to find someplace to work."

"Oh, that's lovely. I'm sure you'll find something you like. Would you be okay with us taking you there?"

Keeping her mace in hand, River took a deep breath and steeled herself. The couple looked harmless, but if not, she always had Nana's small pistol in her backpack. "Sure, if you don't mind."

"Wonderful. Let me help you with your bags." Maybelline took the bigger suitcase and, without any problems, carried it to the truck.

Chester took the bag from his wife and carefully laid it in the bed of his pickup, then turned and smiled at River. "Hello, young lady. Thanks for letting us give you a lift." He took the last bag and put it next to her other one.

"Thank you. I appreciate the ride."

"It's our pleasure." Maybelline patted River's arm. "As we prayed this morning, we knew we were supposed to go for a drive."

Settling in the back seat of their truck, River wasn't sure what to think. Either the people were committed Christians, looney, or something much worse.

"What kind of job are you looking for?" Maybelline asked as Chester drove down the tree-lined road.

"I was thinking of working at a hotel or restaurant," River said.

"Wonderful. Our resident builder, Katherine, is renovating one of our downtown buildings, turning it into a boutique hotel. And, Tiddlywinks Restaurant could probably use another waitress or cook."

Before she could ask why there weren't more places to work in a beach town, Chester stopped at a blinking red light.

On one corner of the street stood a small gas station, and across from that was a volunteer fire department next to a large white-steepled church.

Chester pointed. "That's where we attend. I hope you can join us on Sunday."

"I'll think about it." The only church she'd ever attended was with her friend's family. Her parents never went to church.

As Chester continued driving, River did a double take at the road sign with a cartoon crawdad that read, *Welcome to Crawdad Beach*.

They crossed railroad tracks that looked like they hadn't been used in ages. In the old train station was a public library with a painted mural on the side of a cute cartoon crawdad sitting on a beach reading a book.

Maybelline glanced over her shoulder at River. "I work part-time at the library, so feel free to stop in and get a book once you get settled."

"Thanks." River would probably take the lady up on that offer since she did love to read. Books always gave her a way to escape. She'd miss having access to the school library and Nana's e-reader.

The truck's speed slowed as the road changed from black-top to brick-paved. Two-story brick buildings lined the street, and most even had flowers on their second-floor balconies. They passed a law office, post office, Knick Knacks Antique store, the Curl and Dye Beauty Salon, two buildings with loft apartments, and Doohickeys Hardware.

River couldn't help but grin as she read the sign that Doohickeys, since 1916, had proudly offered a wide range of hardware, building supplies, and whatever whatchamacallit needed.

"Welcome to Crawdad Beach." Chester stopped and parked in front of a place called Tiddlywinks. "I thought you might want something to eat since it's still early." He hurried to open the passenger doors.

River stepped out on the pavement and looked around. The town was really cute.

"Good morning, Chester and Maybelline." A young woman with a lightning bolt shaved in her dark hair waved as she zipped past.

"Good morning, Alexa!" Maybelline called to the lady's retreating back.

An elderly couple walking their little white dog waved at them from across the road. "Good morning!"

Chester and Maybelline returned the greeting.

River couldn't believe how friendly everyone seemed as she started to get her bags from the back of the truck.

Chester hurried toward her. "Don't worry. Your suitcases will be fine while we eat." He motioned with his chin toward a tall, blond-haired man leaning against a lamppost. "That's Gabriel. He's our town's plain clothes policeman."

Maybelline took River by the arm like they were old friends and led her inside the crowded restaurant. "Breakfast will be our treat. Plus, we can check with the owner, Faith Hollis, to see if she has any employment opportunities. I mean, if you're interested."

River nodded with a shrug.

Sitting at a table across from the couple, she picked up a menu with a cute crawdad wearing a chef's hat at the top of the page. The people seemed friendly, and the town had a sense of humor, but was this where she wanted to be? And could she trust people she just met?

Whistling, Sammie Banks strolled along Main Street's sidewalk. He wanted to get to work early to stock the old wooden store shelves for the day. He loved working at Doohickeys Hardware and loved his hometown.

Ever since he was a little kid, he'd worked on the family farm or in town. Doohickeys owner Eric Reed gave Sammie a job when he turned sixteen. Thankfully, his organic farmer parents hadn't pressured him to stay in the family business since his siblings were happy and content working on the farm.

Sammie saved his money, had a 401K, and owned property and a house. His new place needed work, which wasn't a problem since he enjoyed the challenge. Being a Doohickeys employee also gave him a great deal on any building materials he needed.

Since he'd gotten up earlier this morning, he had time to eat breakfast at Tiddlywinks. He usually had a bowl of cereal or a protein bar, but today would probably be busier, and he wanted something more substantial. The town kept a steady stream of visitors since Crawdad Beach had been featured in a famous home and garden magazine.

Sammie entered the restaurant and said hello to people he recognized, which was pretty much everyone there. But one person did not look familiar. He stopped where Chester and Maybelline were sitting and glanced at the nicely tanned blonde who looked close to his age.

Chester stood and shook his hand. "Hey, Sammie. Let me introduce you to River Sawyer. We're trying to convince her to stay in Crawdad Beach."

When River's blue-eyed gaze turned to him, Sammie's thoughts blew away. He'd never seen eyes that color. They were blue, almost gray. Plus, she was gorgeous.

Chester nudged him. "Going to say anything?"

Heat blasting his neck, Sammie tried to get his mind to work. "Oh, yes. Right." He smiled at River. "Welcome to Crawdad Beach. I hope you'll stay."

Uncertainty in her expression, she gave a tentative smile. "Maybe I will."

Hoping that was a positive sign, Sammie grinned. To keep from staring at her, he excused himself and hurried to find an empty table.

He'd stayed busy all his life and hadn't dated other than a few times, but now that he was a homeowner, he liked the idea of finding someone special. Most girls in his high school graduation class had left for college or moved to a bigger city.

Sammie's mom had prayed since he was a little boy for the woman God had for him to marry. He had prayed, too, but he didn't know if that would be a prayer God answered or how long he might have to wait. Either way, he had continued praying and getting his house ready.

Sammie picked up the menu and held it at an angle so he could see over the top and steal a few looks at River.

After meeting her, he'd add to his prayers that she would choose to stay in town.

Chapter 2

"You're offering me a job *and* a place to live?" River stared at Faith Hollis and her husband, George. Why would the owners of Tiddlywinks Restaurant be so quick to do that? First, Chester and Maybelline had picked her up and fed her, and now she'd been offered a job with a place to live.

River tucked a strand of her hair behind her ear. No one knew her. She could be a criminal. Then again, maybe they were dangerous. She shuddered. There were plenty of creepy movies about creepy small towns with overly friendly people.

"Maybelline mentioned you were looking for work, and we could use the extra help." Faith smiled at her. "And if you're looking for a place to stay, you're welcome to use one of our spare bedrooms. We live above the restaurant and have plenty of room."

"You can trust them," Maybelline said with a smile. "You know there might even be an opening in the downtown loft apartments. Or, you could stay in one of our spare bedrooms."

River couldn't decide if she should run screaming or laugh at how crazy this sounded. Total strangers were telling her who to trust and where to live. None of them looked shady. However, some of the shadiest people she knew were adept at hiding their evil tendencies.

However, she did need a job and a place to stay. Since her car couldn't go any further, she needed to do something. "I appreciate your very kind offers, but I'd rather look for somewhere to stay on my own." There was no way she would live in the house of someone she didn't know.

"So, will you take the job?" Faith was almost standing on her tiptoes, leaning toward River with an expectant look.

River took a deep breath. She could do this. "Yes, thank you."

"That's great news. How about you take a few days to settle and start Monday morning? As for a place to live, besides the downtown apartments, the Bowman's duplex is furnished and within walking distance." Faith turned to her husband. "Would you call Julie and ask if we could bring her a possible renter?"

"I'll do that right now," George said, then turned to River and gave her a thumbs up. "Welcome to the Tiddlywinks team." He picked up his cell and made the call.

A furnished duplex? River hoped and prayed that whoever the Bowmans were, they would work with her on the rent. Maybe River could put down a small deposit so she could have enough to pay for a month and then have the rest when she started getting a paycheck.

What was she thinking? Why would they do that? She was a stranger in town, so why would they trust her? River nibbled on a fingernail. She probably had good credit, but could her parents trace her if a credit agency ran it through the system? They probably wouldn't want to find her, but she couldn't take the chance. Maybe she should have changed her name before she left Texas.

If the job worked out and she could afford a place to stay, she had three hundred dollars on the credit card her grandmother had given her. River had already ditched the cheap cell on her parent's plan and bought a pay-as-you-go phone. Only Zachariah and her friend, Lila, knew River's new number.

Maybelline motioned toward the door. "Since Faith and George need to get back to work, I can take you to the duplex." The woman led her outside. "This is so exciting. I hope you enjoyed your breakfast. So, would you like me to drive you or would you like to walk? It's only a few streets over."

River chewed on her fingernail again, then forced her hand to her side. "Since I have my bags, would you mind driving?"

"Of course. Chester's wandered over to Doohickeys to look around, so I get to go with you. Isn't that fun?" Maybelline opened the truck's driver's side door and slid inside. Once River buckled in the passenger seat, Maybelline continued talking. "Our town isn't really on the beach. The ocean is about forty-five minutes away, depending on traffic and the time of year. We're close enough to enjoy the beach but far enough to keep our life here quieter."

River glanced her way. "Then, why is it called Crawdad Beach?"

"The town was established in 1881 and received the name from one of the children who had noticed a crawdad sunning himself on the small sandy riverbank."

At least all the cartoon crawdad signs around town made more sense.

"Sammie's family is a direct descendant of some early settlers," Maybelline added with a grin.

At the mention of the brown-haired guy she'd met at the restaurant, River's cheeks heated. Why would her body react like that? Sammie was cute and seemed nice, but she didn't know him. However, it was good to meet someone closer to her age. Maybe she'd have someone to talk to if she stayed in town. No, she didn't need to let herself think like that. No one would want anything to do with her. Her goal was to find work and start a new life far away from her parents.

A few minutes later, Maybelline parked in front of a sea-green duplex with white shutters and a pretty yard with trees and flowers. Each unit even had a garage, which was a shame since she no longer had a car.

As River exited Maybelline's truck, the right side duplex door opened, and a woman, probably in her forties with sandy brown hair, smiled and hurried toward them.

"River, welcome to our town. I'm Julie Bowman." She motioned for them to follow and called over her shoulder. "Maybelline, I'd love for you to join us." Julie unlocked the door to the unit on the left and led them inside. "The house is fully furnished."

River glanced around at the open living area with light blue walls and plank wood vinyl flooring. Light streamed in from the windows in front and glass French doors in the back.

The den had a soft white couch, a coffee table, two brightly colored floral chairs, and a flat-screen television on a white cabinet. The kitchen and dining area were located at the rear of the room. How could she ever afford something this nice?

Julie pointed to the white-cabinet kitchen and dining area with a round, white-washed wooden table with four chairs. "We have pots, pans, dishes, glasses, and cutlery, and our local grocery store will have any food items you might need." She then guided River to the bedroom, decorated with a light teal bedspread and rattan furniture. White shutter shades covered the windows. The bathroom was decorated with a fun beach motif.

The more River was shown of the duplex, the more tension grew at the base of her neck. A place like this, fully furnished, would cost her more money than she could ever afford.

"There's a laundry area with a stackable washer and dryer," Julie continued. "The remote opener is on the kitchen counter. We also have a security system, cable, and Wi-Fi. I'll show you how to set everything up before I go."

River wanted to dissolve into the floor. Why had she suggested seeing the duplex? "Your place is really nice, but I'm not sure I could afford something like this. I don't have much money."

"Of course, you don't," Julie said, as though situations like this happened daily and were no big deal. "You're young, and you just moved to town. How about you put down a deposit of, let's say, a hundred dollars, if that's okay? Once your job starts, we can decide the best payments for your situation. Let me show you the screened-in porch."

Feeling a little faint, River followed the lady to the screened-in covered patio with flowers spilling out of brightly colored pots.

Maybelline stepped beside her and pointed to the brick house beyond the yard. "We live right behind you. Feel free to come over anytime. I'll make sure you have our cell numbers before I go."

Even though River hadn't told anyone she was willing to rent the place, Julie briefed her on how to set up the security system, gave her the password for the Wi-Fi, and handed her the key to the apartment.

Why were they all being so nice? River took a hundred dollars from her backpack and handed Julie the money. "Thank you for doing this. I can't thank you enough."

"Oh, it's our pleasure. The place has been empty for a few months and needed a new tenant. Once you get your first paycheck, we can draw up paperwork for the rental to make it official. Until then, I hope you enjoy your job and our little town." Julie hugged her and left River standing there, wondering what had happened and how she'd been so lucky.

"River, I'll help you get your bags out of the truck," Maybelline said. "Then, can I drive you to the grocery store to pick up a few things for your new place."

A little shaky in the legs from everything happening so fast, River nodded her thanks.

While at the store, Maybelline introduced her to the people since everyone seemed to know everyone in this town. After returning, River unpacked her groceries and her suitcases, then sat on the couch in her new place. She never thought she'd be able to live in an apartment, or duplex, whatever they called it, that was this nice. Everyone she met was super friendly.

Why?

Why would someone rent a nice place without a copy of a driver's license or some form of identification or complete some paperwork? Wasn't that odd? What if Julie took River's money and then expected her to pay a rent of some crazy high amount? The whole thing happened so fast. Why had she let herself get caught up in the excitement?

Uneasiness slithering up her spine, River jumped to her feet. What if Maybelline and Chester drove the backroads looking for people to kidnap? What if the Hollis's and Julie Bowman and all the rest were part of a plot to lure young women to Crawdad Beach?

Oh, God. What had she done?

Chapter 3

Trying to calm down, River wrapped her arms around herself. She didn't have anyone to call for help since her best friend, Lila, had moved to Atlanta with her family. As for River's parents, they were probably throwing a party that she'd left. They never wanted her, although they would miss using her as a personal maid, house cleaner, and cook.

River paced back and forth. What was she going to do now? Maybe she had watched too many horror movies when she was a kid. She hated that kind of film, but her parents had watched stuff like that and made her sit with them while they laughed when she got afraid.

If it hadn't been for her Christian grandmother, River would never have known God loved her. Nana had been one of the few bright spots in her life. Before she left, Nana had made River promise to leave town and follow wherever God led. Nana even made her memorize the Bible verses in Isaiah 41:10 and Jeremiah 29:11.

To fortify herself, River said the verses out loud, "Do not fear, for I am with you; do not be afraid, for I am your God. I will strengthen you, I will also help you, I will also uphold you with My righteous right hand."

River stopped and looked out the front window at the quiet tree-lined street. "For I know the plans that I have for you, declares the Lord, plans for prosperity and not for disaster, to give you a future and a hope."

As the words washed over her, she took a calming breath. Instead of thinking about a worst-case scenario, she needed to trust God. What if God was behind her coming to Crawdad Beach? What if the people were genuinely nice? She sure hoped that was the case because otherwise, she was in big trouble.

Maybe if she walked around town, she could figure out what was going on. When Maybelline brought her back to the duplex, the streets looked pretty busy, so there might be enough people milling around downtown for River to blend in and no one would notice her.

Placing her backpack on her shoulders, she readied herself. She could do this. She'd keep calm and keep her ears and eyes open. If she were in danger, she'd call the police, FBI, CIA, and the National Guard.

Speaking of calling someone, she probably should let Lila know where she was now. River placed the call, and thirty minutes later, her friend told her she was on the way. Maybe River shouldn't have told her what was happening. She'd tried to talk her friend out of coming, but since Lila's dad was on the board of directors for a major airline and her mom worked as a Vice President for a rental car company, she wouldn't take no for an answer.

River sighed. She probably should have gone with Lila and her family when they moved to Georgia, but River couldn't leave behind her grandmother. Now that Nana was gone, maybe River should have driven to Atlanta instead of winding up here. Then again, what would have happened if the car died while she was on a major freeway?

Well, she couldn't change things now, but what she could do was put on her sunglasses and go into spy mode. River chuckled; there was no way a little town like this would have spies. That fact would work in her favor. She would use the stealth mode she perfected growing up in a house where her presence wasn't wanted.

Locking the door behind her, River stepped out front and surveyed her surroundings. Birds twilled in the tree branches as though they didn't have a care in the world. She walked the tree-lined street with well-maintained older houses, some of which had been updated.

Turning the corner, she casually strolled on the downtown sidewalk. Although Crawdad Beach wasn't very big, it was busy. River turned at the sound of a lawnmower and almost ran into a streetlamp.

Hunched over the wheel of a riding lawnmower like street racing, a woman wearing a bright fuchsia velveteen jogging suit chugged down the street. People waved and greeted the lady as though her presence was an everyday occurrence.

After watching the lady drive away, River stopped at Knick Knack's Antique Store and peeked in the front window. The older building was crowded with all sorts of interesting-looking items. As she stepped inside, a little bell hanging over the door dinged.

"Good morning!" A young woman with long brunette hair and big brown eyes stood next to a tall, brown-haired, good-looking guy with a well-trimmed beard.

River gave a little wave at the couple.

"Let us know if we can help you find anything," the guy said with a smile.

River nodded, then wandered through the store filled with glassware, art, old toys, antique jewelry, and antique and repurposed furniture. She sidestepped a group of older women excitedly discussing a piece of furniture.

River spotted a stained glass sign that pointed to a book nook. She loved reading. Nestled in wood shelves that seemed to be from another time sat two chairs on either side of an old floor lamp. River ran her hand along the shelves of old and newer-looking books. Life was hard, and the world seemed to be crashing around her, so besides reading the Bible, she loved escaping into a fictional world with a happy-ever-after ending.

She chose two novels that looked entertaining. One was a Western about women who wanted to become Pinkerton agents, and the other was about a group of women in the late 1800s who started an investigation agency. The books sounded perfect for her situation.

Hopefully, when Lila arrived, they would become agents and investigate Crawdad Beach.

Chester stood next to Maybelline, peeling potatoes at their kitchen sink. "I talked to Chief Weaver. He said they found a burnt-out car on the road where we found River. He's also looking into any reports of any missing persons that might meet her description."

"Oh, dear. A burnt-out car doesn't sound good. Do you think River's a runaway?" Maybelline cut up the potatoes and gave them a good cold water rinse before placing them in a pan.

"I'm not sure, but I believe she's running from something or someone."

"Poor baby. River did have a cautious look about her as if she wasn't sure who to trust. She reminded me of some of the foster kids we took in over the years."

Chester nodded. "You're right, or like Marie had when she first moved here."

"Well, hopefully, River isn't in witness protection like Marie had been." Maybelline set the pan on the stove and turned toward him. "I'm grateful Faith gave River a job, and Julie agreed to let her stay. I told Julie we would make up any difference in money she might lose renting the place at such a low rate, but she said not to worry. She'd take care of that and keep an eye on River to make sure she's safe."

"Since Julie's husband is the mayor who also owns a software security company, River is in good hands. Now we need to figure out what else we can do to help the girl."

"Do you think we came on a little strong giving River a job and an apartment without questioning who she was or getting references? I hope she knows we have good intentions."

"Me too," Chester said. "Otherwise, she might be worried."

His soft-hearted wife got a little teary-eyed. "I hate thinking River might be afraid, especially of us and our little town. I'm going to alert the CBPT."

"Good idea since the Crawdad Beach prayer team is the best place to cover our new little girl." He smiled at his wife.

How he loved his woman. They'd been married for decades, and their love continued to grow. Chester put his arms around her and gave her a big kiss.

Maybelline squirmed out of his embrace and gave him a saucy look. "Chester Taylor, we need to continue that discussion later."

Chester wiggled his eyebrows. "I'm looking forward to that. I *love* our discussions."

She giggled as she sashayed out of the kitchen.

Now, back to the task at hand. He had no doubt the good Lord brought River to their town, and by golly, they would do their best to protect the young woman and make her feel comfortable.

Chapter 4

"Is this the store where they found a treasure?"

River's ears perked up. *Treasure?* She hurried to where a group of older women stood, staring expectantly at the couple behind the counter.

The guy chuckled. "Yes, it belonged to a distant relative. The store's original owner, Flornoy Bounds, had hidden it to keep it safe for his family." He pointed to an old photo.

River smiled at the mischievous grin on the man's face in the picture. Most people back then didn't usually have any expression on their faces other than stern or bland.

"Oh, how exciting!" One woman said. Her friends nodded in agreement and continued asking questions about the treasure and what was found.

"If you're ready, I can check you out." The brunette behind the counter motioned toward River.

Maybe while the other women were occupied, this was the chance she needed to ask a few questions of her own. She laid her books on the counter and gave a pleasant smile. "Is Crawdad Beach a nice place?"

"It's the best. I've lived here most of my life and wouldn't want to be anywhere else."

River handed her the money to cover the cost for her books. Would it be good that the lady lived here that long, or would that mean she'd be part of covering up anything seedy?

The lady tilted her head. "Are you thinking of living here?"

River shrugged. "Maybe."

"I hope you'll join us. I'm Grace Johnson, and this is my husband, Jeremy." Grace smiled at her husband as she squeezed his arm. He gave her a quick grin, then turned his attention back to what River's grandmother used to call a gaggle of females as they continued asking questions about the treasure.

After thanking Grace, River stepped back on the sidewalk. So far, she'd learned the antique store had a treasure, and the couple that ran the place seemed nice enough. But still, she needed to keep asking questions to discover the truth.

River walked under a teal and white awning over the door of Rolling in the Dough Bakery, stepped inside, and breathed deep some very yummy smells. People of various ages and races sat around bistro tables, talking together, drinking coffee, or eating pastries.

She grinned at the mural of a cute cartoon crawdad holding a rolling pin in one of his claws and an oven mitt in the other. On the other wall was an older-looking bicycle with a basket, and across from that was a display cabinet of what looked like old-timey bakery tools.

River stepped to the glass front display cases.

Her mouth started watering as she checked out all the goodies they offered.

A young woman with light brown hair and dark brown eyes smiled. "Can I get you anything?"

"What is a crawdad claw?" River pointed to a pastry and sent a questioning glance at the woman.

"Well, most places call it a bear claw, but since we're in Crawdad Beach, we call it a crawdad claw."

River grinned. "It looks good. Could I have one, please? And some water?"

"Of course." The woman placed the pastry on a plate, handed her a water bottle, and told her the cost. "So, are you visiting our town?"

"I might work at the restaurant."

"That's great. I'm Olivia Paterson. I grew up in Houston, but Crawdad Beach is now home. I love it here. I hope you do, too."

River thanked her, paid for the purchase, and then sat at a little table by the front window. *Loving a home.* What a strange thought. Would she ever feel that way anywhere she lived?

Trying not to be obvious, River kept her ears open to listen to the conversations around her. At a table on her right, a middle-aged guy scrolled on his phone while sipping his coffee.

At the table to her left, two older women discussed a book they were reading. "It reminds me of what Marie must have gone through when she moved here," said the woman with salt and pepper hair.

"You're right." An attractive black woman said. "I can't imagine being in witness protection."

River tried not to lean their way to hear the rest of that discussion. Witness protection? How interesting.

A high-pitched nasally voice at the table behind her made her cringe.

"You know who I'm talking about," said a scowling, large-chested woman sitting with a younger woman. "Wilder Templeton, he was the man who saved the bakery from the bomb."

River tried not to jerk her head around. Did she say bomb?

"I remember, Mother." The blonde-haired woman wore jeans and a way-too-tight red top. Her false eyelashes and heavy makeup didn't hide the fact that she wasn't as young as she dressed. "It's such a shame he married that spy lady. Wilder does look like an older Sean Connery."

"He is a handsome man. But don't worry, Belle. There is someone out there worthy of you."

The younger woman, apparently named Belle, hmphed as she tapped her painted red fingernails on the table. "Men don't understand *all* that I have to offer."

Her mother patted Belle's hand. "The right one hasn't come along, but he's out there. You'll find someone wealthy who wants to spoil you the way you deserve to be spoiled."

River tried not to gag. Money didn't solve anything. Her dad had a good income, which caused more problems than she could list.

Her parents never saved a penny, and their credit cards stayed maxed to the limit since her mother's favorite sport was shopping for herself. When her dad was home from business trips, if they weren't throwing wild parties, they'd leave River at home and fly to beach resorts.

Sighing from the depressing thoughts, River refocused on the moment. What was the deal about a bomb, a spy lady, and someone else who had been in witness protection? Plus, the antique store had a treasure.

Who would have thought a small town like this would be so interesting?

"Sammie, do you know our inventory on eight-penny exterior galvanized smooth shank common nails?" Gloria, with her sparkling brown eyes and milk chocolate complexion, walked toward him.

Proud that he knew the answer since Gloria was in charge of accounting and purchasing for the store, he grinned at the woman he considered his second mom. "On our two and a half by quarter inch nails, we have fifteen one-pound boxes. Is that what you need?"

She returned his smile. "I knew I could count on you. During that little power surge we had earlier, our software glitched as I was entering data."

"Well, hello, you two." Chester Taylor came toward them. "What's happening today in Doohickey world?"

Sammie shook his outstretched hand. "Staying busy as usual."

Chester hugged Gloria. "You're looking mighty fine this morning."

Gloria grinned. "Thank you, kind sir. Tell Maybelline hello for me. And don't forget you're both coming to dinner next weekend at our place."

"We will be there and looking forward to it. But, this time, I won't be so easy on you when we play dominoes. You and your hubby won the last six times, but I'm feeling lucky."

"Ha. You wish. I'll see you later." Gloria chuckled as she walked away.

"What are you up to today?" Sammie asked Chester.

"Maybelline and I went for a drive this morning where we found River and brought her back with us."

Sammie held up his hand before Chester could continue. "Wait. What do you mean you found River?"

"She was walking along the side of the road with a couple of suitcases. Nobody was around, so we asked if we could drive her here."

"Didn't she have a car?"

"We didn't see one. But, Chief later found a burnt-out vehicle further down that road. Must have been hers."

"River's car burnt up? Didn't she have anyone to call?"

"That's a good question." Chester rubbed his chin. "I should have asked. Either way, we brought her here. She'll start working at Tiddlywinks on Monday and live in the Bowman duplex."

"That's good, but was she on her way here or somewhere else?"

"Not sure," Chester said. "River said she planned to work at a hotel or restaurant by the beach."

"We aren't on the beach."

"Nope, but we have a restaurant, and the hotel is almost finished," Chester said as though it made perfect sense.

Sammie was okay with Chester's thinking. Whatever had happened, having someone as cute as River working at Tiddlywinks would be nice. He might have to visit there a lot more often.

"Anyway," Chester said. "I'm helping Jeremy repurpose furniture for his shop this afternoon, and I need more sandpaper and another gallon of paint stripper. We found an old dresser that will take a lot of work."

The bell over the front door signaled another customer had arrived.

Chester chuckled, "We are going to strip her bare and go from there."

Sammie turned to see who had come inside the building.

River, seemingly frozen in place, stood at the end of the aisle with a horrified expression on her face.

Chapter 5

As much as she wanted to run, River's feet seemed glued to the store's floor. They were going to strip her? She knew it, the town seemed nice on the outside, but inside, they were horrible monsters.

"Well, hello!" Chester said as he walked toward her

Her breath caught in her throat. She held up her hands to stop him.

He paused and sent her a confused look. "Are you okay?"

Her feet finally felt like they could move, so she backed away. "No! Get away from me."

Chester scratched his head and glanced over at Sammie. "Do you know what's going on?"

Sammie shrugged, then took a step toward her. "Can I help you?"

He looked nice enough, but she didn't know who she could trust. Chester already knew where she was staying. Were they going to come after her later tonight? Was Sammie part of what was going on, or could she trust him?

Not wanting to take a chance, she bolted for the door and ran back to the duplex as fast as she could. Gasping for air, she locked herself inside and set the alarm. At least she had some security.

Raking her hand through her hair, River paced back and forth. She should never have gotten in Chester's truck, never have agreed to a job at that restaurant, or taken a duplex next to people she probably couldn't trust. What was she going to do now?

She didn't have anywhere to go, and Lila wouldn't be here until later tonight. The windows that looked so inviting earlier now looked like portals for people to break in and attack her.

River ran to the bedroom and threw all her belongings in her suitcases. She would *not* stay here. Once Lila arrived, she'd get her to take her somewhere far away. Atlanta was looking better by the minute.

"What was that about?"

Sammie shrugged at Chester's question. "I haven't a clue." Hopefully, River wasn't looking at him with that expression. Sammie tried to look presentable now that he was twenty-one and even made sure he had a more professional-looking haircut. He hoped someday to become the store manager.

Chester rubbed the back of his neck. "What were we talking about when River came into the store?"

"You were telling me about some dresser you would strip."

Chester's tan face turned a shade lighter. "Oh, no. Do you think she heard me talking about stripping something, and she thought it was her?"

Sammie felt his eyebrows hike to his hairline. "*Why* would she think something like that? Man, that's an extremely disturbing thought."

"Yes, it is," Chester said. "If River thought that, she's got to be terrified."

Sammie gulped. He hated to see anyone scared. "That would be awful. So, what are you going to do?"

"I'm not sure. Maybe I can get Maybelline over to River's place to reassure her."

"If River thinks you're going to do something terrible to her, I doubt she would trust your wife."

"Good point. Especially since we're the ones who found River on the side of the road."

"Explain to me again about finding River."

"This morning, Maybelline and I prayed and felt like we should drive the back roads. That's when we saw River walking alone with her backpack and two suitcases. There wasn't a car anywhere, so we didn't know if her vehicle had broken down or someone dropped her off. We picked her up and took her to Tiddlywinks for breakfast. Faith offered her a job, and Julie gave her a place to stay at her duplex."

Sammie grimaced. "Okay, that sounds nice, but to someone who's not a Crawdadian, that might seem a little off-the-chart friendly. If River's all alone, and strangers pick her up and give her a job and a place to stay, it sounds like the plot of a creepy movie."

Chester groaned. "Maybelline mentioned we might have come on a little strong, but I didn't think about it being like a scary movie. Well, we better think of something fast because if what we're thinking is what she's thinking, she's got to be scared out of her little mind."

"Based on River's expression, I'd say she is totally freaked out."

"What's going on?" Gloria asked as she came toward them. "You two look like something terrible has happened."

Chester took a few minutes to explain the situation.

Gloria gasped. "Oh my goodness, that poor girl. Something needs to be done to put her mind at ease."

"We agree, but what?" Sammie asked.

"Oh, dear. If you go to River's place, she might worry that you're coming after her. But, if you don't straighten everything out, there is no telling what she will do."

"What a mess," Chester said. "We were trying to be good people, and all we did was scare the poor girl to death. Who in town might be able to help?"

"We could call the pastor," Gloria said.

"True, but River doesn't know the preacher. Why would she trust him? Maybe we could call Chief Weaver or Gabriel?" Sammie offered.

"She doesn't know the police, but maybe if they come in their cruiser, she would be okay with that. I know," Chester snapped his fingers. "What about Marie? She was in witness protection, so maybe she'd know how to talk to River."

Sammie shook his head. "Again, we have the problem that River doesn't know anyone and doesn't know who to trust."

Chester sighed. "Well, we can't stand here and do nothing. I'm calling the Chief to explain the situation and see what he advises."

Gloria nodded. "I'll call the CBPT about this too. This is serious."

"You should have gotten a CPBT text earlier."

"I haven't checked my phone since I've been at work."

"No worries, they've already started praying for her, but tell them the latest while I call the Chief." Chester took his phone out of his back pocket and made the call.

Sammie sent up a prayer for River. He didn't know her, but he hoped that once they straightened everything out, she would stay in Crawdad Beach.

If River thought the townspeople were trying to harm her, how could anyone convince her she was safe?

Chapter 6

River said goodbye to Chief Weaver and Gabriel, locked her door, and reset the alarm. The officers had tried to reassure her that she was safe and the people in Crawdad Beach were only being friendly, but she still worried that the police could also be involved. What if they wanted her to relax and not worry, and then when she least expected it, they would attack?

Her phone signaled an incoming text. River groaned as she read that Lila wouldn't arrive until about ten o'clock. That meant several more hours before her friend would get here. Waiting was the pits.

She probably needed to eat something since she hadn't had anything since breakfast. River went to the kitchen and looked at what she had bought at the store. One of her many responsibilities growing up had been to cook for the family. Her mom would have River prepare the meals, and then when her dad came home, her mom would pretend she had made the meal, and River didn't help. Groaning, she shook off the thought.

Thank goodness she had bought a pop-in-the-microwave dish from the store. She wasn't exactly hungry, but if she didn't eat, she did tend to get more dramatic than usual.

It's not that she was a drama-type person, but she could get a little weepy when hungry. She popped the food in and leaned against the kitchen counter.

So, exactly when was the last time she had a healthy meal? Besides this morning, it had probably been about two weeks since anything decent entered her stomach—no wonder she felt overwhelmed.

She wasn't even sure her thoughts were typical for someone her age since most of her time had been spent with her grandmother or Lila. Her friend wasn't an average teenager with her off-the-chart I.Q. and had even graduated high school with enough credits for a third-year college-level status.

River had made somewhat decent grades but not enough for a college scholarship. Her parents never spent money on her, so going away to a university was out of the question. They had raised River to be their housekeeper, cook, laundry woman, and gardener. River hmphed. They wouldn't miss her, but they would miss the free labor.

The microwave beeped, signaling the meal was ready. Forcing her thoughts away from the past, River took the food to the table, said a prayer, and finished in no time. Obviously, she was hungrier than she thought.

She felt a little more human and not quite as worried, but then she noticed it was getting dark.

Jumping to her feet, she checked the door locks, closed the curtains and blinds, and ensured the alarm was set and working.

As a final measure, River grabbed her mace and Nana's pistol, then sat on the couch where she would wait for her friend.

Wishing he had a gavel to pound on a podium, Chester whistled to quiet the crowd. "Okay, people, we have a situation on our hands. Quiet down so we can continue the meeting." He surveyed his friends and neighbors gathered in the lobby of the soon-to-be hotel. "As I explained earlier, we need to figure out how to ensure River knows she is safe and welcome in our little town."

His friend, Henry, held up his hand. "Maybe we could have some of the women take River a welcome to Crawdad Beach basket."

"Great idea," David, Henry's grandson, said. "I did that when Marie first moved to town."

His wife, Marie, kissed David's cheek. "And it was an adorable thing for you to do." The couple stared at each other all lovey-dovey.

"I like that idea," Maybelline agreed. "I could make her a small cake."

Olivia patted Maybelline's arm. "That's so sweet of you, Maybelline. But, we have plenty of pastries we can take her from the bakery."

"Oh, good point. I'll think of something else."

Grace held up her hand. "River came into Knick Knacks and bought a couple of books. I could take her the next ones in that series."

Grace's husband, Jeremy, nodded. "That's a great idea. I could look around the store and see if we have anything else to add to the gift basket."

"Oh, goodie," Julie Bowman said. "I can take her a bouquet of flowers."

"I could give her a free haircut," the Curl and Dye Beauty shop owner added.

"Do you think she needs any hardware or tools?" Eric asked.

Sammie grinned. "I could maybe go over and ask her."

More people shouted out what they could take River.

Chester sighed. Things were getting out of hand. Poor River wouldn't have enough space to fit everything they were bringing her.

A piercing whistle quieted everyone.

Chief Weaver moved to the front. "Fellow Crawdadians, we need to be cautious not to add additional worry to River. When Gabriel and I talked to her this afternoon, she was suspicious of us and the town. The sad truth is that our world has many problems, and trusting people can be an issue. Many of us have lived here most of our lives and can easily accept kindness."

"Unfortunately, out there," he motioned with his hand, "it's not that way." Chief's gaze moved from Marie, Stella, Wilder, Mia, and several other newcomers to town. "I know those of you who haven't been with us as long understand. Evil exists and seems to be growing by the minute. Therefore, let's be kind and loving and take things much slower with River."

Henry came next to the Chief. "I agree. Swamping her with gifts could be overwhelming."

"Well," Yvonne Cowman scowled as she crossed her arms over her ample chest. "I, for one, think the whole thing is ridiculous. We don't know anything about this girl. She might have come to town to cause trouble."

"I agree, Mother," her daughter, Belle, wearing her typical too-tight clothing, nodded. "We don't know who River is, so why are you all making such a big deal about her? We've had new people move to town before."

Chief's eyebrow raised as he leveled his gaze on the women. "We *will* be kind to the young woman." He turned his gaze back to the others. "Since River mentioned a friend of hers will be arriving tonight, let's give them space. Maybe when River and her friend venture out of the duplex, we can show love to them both."

"I vote for that," Chester said.

Except from Mrs. Cowman and Belle, murmurs of agreement came from the rest.

"I still would love to take her some welcome gifts." A woman at the back of the room shouted. "Me too," came another voice.

Chester cut his eyes to the Chief and shrugged. "Well, we tried. Even if River leaves us, she will leave well-gifted and well-loved."

Chapter 7

"So, what do you think?" River chewed on her fingernail as she stood in front of her friend.

Lila adjusted her glasses, then smoothed a hand over her dark hair. "Well, you either have an incredibly active imagination, or you are in the middle of a very disturbing situation."

"I know, right?" River sat next to her. "Crawdad Beach is one of the nicest places on the planet or should be featured on a documentary about the creepiest town ever."

Lila rubbed her earlobe, a sign she was in deep thought, and then leaned toward River. "So, let me get this straight. Someone offered you a ride after your car exploded, then someone else offered you a job, and someone else gave you a nice place to live for hardly any money, which made you realize the people were out to get you?"

River avoided looking at her friend. "It doesn't sound as scary when you say it," she muttered. "But it's not just that. What about what I heard Chester say about . . ." she took a deep breath, "stripping her."

"Where were you when you overheard him?"

"In a hardware store."

Lila tilted her head. "You mean those places where people get tools for projects like refinishing furniture?"

Heat enveloped River's body. Had she got everything wrong? Oh. My. Goodness. Were the people in this town just nice?

"All those horror movies your parents made you watch may have affected your thinking. Tell you what." Lila stood and pulled River to her feet. "Let's get some sleep, and tomorrow, I'll go with you to investigate the town."

River nodded. What if all her worries were because of her overactive imagination? "I'm sorry I called you if everything is okay. And if it's not, I don't want to put you in danger."

"Hey, that's what friends are for." Lila gave her a quick hug. "Tomorrow, we'll go on an expedition to find the truth. Either we will call the FBI, or this will become one of your more embarrassing moments."

River had tossed, turned, and worried most of the night. The next morning, she groaned as she wrapped her robe around her and shuffled through the family room on her way to the kitchen.

Lila had already folded up the blankets where she'd slept on the couch. Her friend was already showered and dressed and stood frowning in front of the open refrigerator. "You don't have much to eat."

"Sorry. I just got here yesterday. Since Maybelline drove me to the store, I didn't want to take too long, so I only got a few things."

"Maybelline?" Lila raised an eyebrow. "She's the lady with Chester that picked you up on the side of the road. So the woman fed you, found you a job, then took time out of her day to drive you here and to the store?"

River sighed at how things sounded when Lila said them. "Yes."

"I can see why you've been scared."

River narrowed her eyes at her friend. "You weren't here, so don't be all judgmental about what happened and how I felt."

"I'm sorry." Lila held up a hand. "You've had a crummy life, so I understand why you have trouble trusting people. You mentioned a bakery. Why don't we get something to eat after you get ready? My treat."

"No, I'll buy since you were nice enough to come here."

Lila stared at her. "How much money do you have?"

Knowing she had no choice but to answer truthfully, River avoided looking at her friend. "Three hundred on the credit card and a little less than four hundred since I went to the store and put a down payment on the apartment."

"That's *all* you have? What happened to the money you had in your account?"

River grimaced. "Mother took it since she was on the bank's signature card."

Lila sucked in a breath. "She withdrew *your* money?"

"Yes, all of it. The cash I have with me is what I had hidden at the house."

Lila's face turned red as she fisted her hands. "That's robbery! That money was what your grandmother gave to you, not to them."

"I know, but what can I do? I didn't find out Mother had taken the money until the day I left." River shouldn't have been surprised since her parents had supposedly sold her grandmother's house for Nana's care but instead had bought themselves two new cars and redone their kitchen.

Muttering under her breath, Lila shook her head. "I'm sorry, River. I'm sorry you have such lousy parents. I've never understood why they adopted you. Please let me help you with some money."

"No," Trying not to cry, River backed away. "I can do this." She *had* to make it on her own.

"I don't doubt you can do it, but why don't you come home with me? Please. You're my best friend, and my family loves you."

"But you'll be away at college and have a boyfriend, so what would I do? Stay at your parent's house while they go to their jobs? I don't even have a car now. At least if I stay here, I can walk to work."

Lila groaned a growl. "I hate this. I wish I could go back in time and fix everything for you. I wish you'd been born into my family."

"Aw, that would have been nice. But I wasn't, and I can't change that." Trying not to cry, River stared at the floor. Why wasn't her life different?

"River, you are smart, kind, loving, and beautiful. Don't ever forget those facts."

River snorted. "Sounds like something said in a movie."

"Whether or not a movie stole my line, it's true. I am so ready for something good to happen for you. God does good things for His children, and you are *way* overdue for some good stuff. Speaking of good, let's go to that bakery. I need something sweet and sugary to get my blood pumping."

River took a quick shower, dressed, grabbed her backpack, and led Lila out the door.

Things didn't seem as creepy having her friend with her and it being a new day. Puffy white clouds floated in the blue sky, birds were chirping, and flowers were blooming.

Staying in step with her friend, River glanced her way. "You should try the crawdad claws when we get to the bakery."

Lila gave her a disgusted look. "Crawdad claws?"

"It's like a bear claw but in the shape of a crawdad." River tapped her fingers together.

"Okay, that's interestingly creative. The town does seem to embrace its namesake. Where do you want to go after we finish eating?"

"I guess we can stop by the antique store and then go to Doohickeys. I haven't been to the beauty shop since I don't need a haircut. Maybe we could think of a reason to stop in to see if they have any gossip we could overhear. And we could stop by Tiddlywinks restaurant for lunch. There's also a park right past downtown."

"The place sounds pretty idyllic for a small town." Lila grinned.

"Maybe," River said. "But I need to be sure."

"No problem. I'm here until Sunday night. Then, I need to get back for class. That is unless you really need me. I won't leave you if we find out anything bad. Because if we do, I'm taking you home with me. Mom and Dad said not to leave unless you're safe."

River's lip trembled at the thought of Lila's sweet parents. "They've always been good to me."

"I'm sorry we couldn't do more. We knew you would stay once your grandmother came to live with you."

"As hard as everything was, I'm grateful I got to spend those years with her." River had been thirteen when Nana came to live with them. Getting up early, River would cook and care for her grandmother, go to school, run home to take care of the house, clean, and cook. She didn't mind the time spent with Nana, but River had basically been a prisoner in her own home.

"Your grandmother was a mischievous and very cool woman," Lila said. "I hate that she was pretty much bedridden after that motorcycle accident, but without her there, there is no telling what might have happened to you. Her presence at least provided some protection, especially during your parent's wild parties."

"True. As much as I hated being locked in the bedroom with Nana, it did keep us safer. But, cleaning up after those parties was a nightmare." River cringed at the memories of loud music, horrible language, the smell of alcohol, cigarettes, and the odor from other non-tobacco products.

"I'm sorry you had to put up with all of that. I know you still miss your grandmother, but I'm grateful you left when you did. It still makes me sick that your parents pretended to be upstanding citizens of our town and that your dad could even keep working with their partying lifestyle."

River shrugged and stopped in front of the bakery. "Our house was far enough from other people that most didn't know what was really going on. Since Dad's job is based in Dallas, they probably don't have a clue what he's really like."

"Well, let's hope you get a new start now."

Praying it would be true, River peeked into the bakery window to see if it was crowded.

Sammie carried Ms. Norma's purchases to her car and placed the bag in her back seat. "Are you sure you don't need me to go with you to unload it?"

"No, thank you, Sammie. That's sweet of you." The elderly widow patted his arm. "My neighbor is working in his yard today, so he will come over to help if I need him."

"Okay, if you're sure."

"I'll be fine." With a few groans, she got settled in the driver's seat.

"Have a good day, Ms. Norma. Make sure you call me if you need anything."

"I will do that."

Sammie shut her car door and watched as though in slow motion, she pulled away.

He had a soft spot for the widows in town and tried to help however he could. Fortunately, most of the Crawdadians looked after one another. Sammie took a look around the street, and his heart rate jumped. River and her friend were standing in front of the bakery. Should he go see her? Would that be too much? He shot a glance at the store, then back to the bakery. Maybe Eric and Gloria would cover for him for a few minutes. He could even offer to pick up something for them. Yes, that would work.

Sammie ran inside and found Eric. "Would you mind if I went to the bakery for a few minutes?"

"Sure, as long as you get me a cinnamon roll and check to see if Gloria wants something."

"Will do." He hurried toward her. "Can I get you anything from Rolling in the Dough?"

"Thanks for the offer, but nothing for me. I had a big breakfast." She grinned at him. "You're looking rather bright-eyed. Would a certain young woman perhaps be at the bakery this morning?"

Heat crawling up his neck, he grinned. "Maybe."

Gloria chuckled. "Go and have fun. I'll cover for you."

"Thanks." Sammie bounded out of the store and ran toward the bakery. He didn't see River, so maybe they were inside.

Lifting up a prayer that he wouldn't do anything stupid, he skidded to a stop and tried to act casual.

Chapter 8

"Hi, River!"

Pausing in the bakery's doorway, River tried to figure out how many people had greeted her by name. How did they know her? Everywhere she looked, people were smiling at her like she was a rockstar.

Lila nudged her. "Must be nice to be so popular."

Ignoring her friend's comment, River gave a little wave to those sitting at the tables and hurried to the counter.

"Good morning, River," Olivia said with a big smile. "Who's your friend?"

River introduced Lila to the bakery owner.

"Nice to meet you, Lila. I hope you enjoy your time in Crawdad Beach."

"Thanks. Seems like a pretty nice place, and everybody is friendly."

Olivia got a dreamy-eyed look. "It's the best place on earth with great people. So, what can I get you both?"

After placing their order, River and her friend sat at a table by the front window.

Lila put a napkin on her lap, took a big bite of her cinnamon roll, and moaned in pleasure. "These are great."

Wiping a smear of icing off her lips, River nodded. "This is the absolute best cinnamon roll I have ever had."

Her friend leaned toward her. "So, how do all these people know you?"

River raised her shoulders. "I have no clue." It was weird but nice. Back in Texas, hardly anyone knew her outside of school.

The bakery door opened, and Sammie stepped inside. His gaze scanned the room, paused on her, and he grinned.

For some strange reason, her cheeks heated again. River looked away and took another bite of her roll. She needed to refocus. She was supposed to find out what the people were like, not stare at a cute guy.

"Well, who is that?" Lila gave her a mischievous grin.

"His name is Sammie. He works over at Doohickeys."

"He's cute. And from the look on his face when he spotted you, he's interested in getting to know you better."

"Shh," River held her finger to her mouth and whispered. "That's the guy that was with Chester talking about . . . you know doing that . . . thing."

"Oh. Since Sammie blushed and looked flustered as he smiled at you, I don't think he's the kind you need to worry about."

"Some of the worst people in history looked like decent people."

Lila motioned with her eyes for River to look at something.

Holding a sack of bakery items, Sammie took a halting step toward their table. "Hi."

River looked up at his very cute face. "Hi." What else was she supposed to say?

He swallowed. "Um, I hope you're having a good day."

"Yeah, it's okay."

"Good. That's good. Hey, if you ever need anything, I work at the hardware store."

"Right. Thanks. I think I have everything I need for now."

"Oh. Okay. Well, I hope you and your friend have a good day."

"Thanks. You, too."

He turned and left in a hurry.

Lila glanced at her. "After that awkward interaction, I would cross Sammie off your suspect list. The only thing the guy seems guilty of is drooling over you. And wipe that surprised look off your face. You're super-cute."

"Super-cute? Right. That's why I've only had two dates in my life."

"The only reason you haven't dated is because you were always stuck at home."

River cringed at that truth. Besides Lila and a few people at school, River never had much of a social life. Most of what she knew about romance was from the books she read or from movies. She was eighteen and had only been kissed once, and that kiss had been from a boy she liked in elementary school during recess.

The girls in her high school gym class used to make fun of her, saying River would be the only attendee in a virgin convention. She might not have a love life, but at least she could read about romance.

Lila nudged her foot with hers. "Before you get all depressed on me, why don't we explore the town?"

Four and a half hours later, River and Lila made their way back to her place. They had visited the stores, ate lunch at Tiddlywinks, walked to the park, and followed the trail along a lazy river. Everywhere they went, people greeted River and wanted to meet Lila. It was like River had lived here all her life and was part of the town.

Lila nudged her with her elbow. "This really is a nice place to live. I haven't seen anything that makes me think the place is scary."

"Yeah, I agree." River sighed. "I guess I overreacted. People are friendly, but you think it's genuine?"

"Seems to be. The town stays busy with visitors. I think if something bad were going on, they'd probably keep closed off. Maybe you were freaked out because Crawdad Beach is so different from the rest of the world. It's like a little oasis in a sea of trouble.

"Maybe so. You think I should stay here and give it a try?"

A calico cat walked toward them and purred as he rubbed their legs. They pet his soft fur, and his purr increased.

"I'd love for you to come back with me," Lila said, "but if you want to make it on your own, this might be a good place to settle. But promise you'll call me if you ever need me, okay?"

"I will. Thanks." Maybe she had a shot at having a decent life after all.

Monday morning, she'd start a new job and a new life. She'd never been a waitress before, but how hard could it be since she'd waited on her parents all her life? Faith had also told River she could help in the kitchen if that would be more comfortable. She did know how to cook. She'd watched cooking shows most of her life, so at least she had some good options.

Things were finally looking up. River turned to head down her street, and her stomach dropped.

Sitting in front of her duplex was a police car with two officers inside.

Chapter 9

Frustrated at his lack of communication skills when he'd seen River at the bakery, Sammie groaned. It wasn't like he hadn't talked to females before. He usually didn't have any trouble, but with River, he turned into a blubbering idiot.

Between working at the store, taking college courses, helping his parents and others during his off hours, and church on Sunday, he didn't have time for women. Obviously, this had become a problem. He had dated before and even at one time had a steady girlfriend, so why was he having trouble now?

Besides River being beautiful, something about her made him want to be with her and protect her. She reminded him of a wild, scared rabbit he had rescued when he was younger. He wasn't a big football-looking type guy, but he was strong and wouldn't hesitate to help someone in trouble.

"Hey, Sammie!" Chester's voice came from another aisle. "Could you give me a hand?"

"On my way." He turned the corner and found Chester halfway in the wooden whatchamacallit bin, searching for something.

Chester glanced at him and held up a rusty part. "I need a whatchamacallit like this. It's from an antique chandelier that looks like it was probably from the 1800s. Jeremy is converting it from gas to electric. They don't make anything like this now, so I hoped to find a part we could use in here."

Sammie got on his knees and helped him look.

"Have you seen River today?" Chester asked.

"Yeah, for a few minutes at the bakery. She had a friend with her. We didn't talk long."

"Did River seem okay? I hope she realizes we were only trying to help."

"She looked terrific. I mean, she looked okay. I'm not sure if she's thinking about still staying, but I hope she starts trusting us." He hoped God had brought River to their town and that she would let him in her life, whether as a friend or more than a friend.

Either way, he didn't want River to be scared of the town or afraid of him.

"Come in." River hoped the policemen didn't hear the quiver in her voice as she stepped aside to let them inside. She cast a quick glance at Lila, who looked as troubled and scared as River felt.

The silver-haired police chief cleared his throat. "River, I need to ask you a few questions. First off, how old are you?"

Her throat tightened at his serious expression. Why would he ask that? "I'm eighteen."

He wrote something down on a small pad before his intense gaze settled back on her face. "On the road where Chester and Maybelline found you, there was a burnt-out car. Do you know anything about that?"

She sat on the couch before her legs gave out. "Yes, sir. That was mine."

"Why didn't you tell anyone about the car?" Gabriel asked.

River nibbled on her lip. "I didn't know what to do. The car kind of exploded, so I left it there. I'm sorry. I guess maybe I should have said something to someone, but who would I have called? I didn't know anyone in the area."

"I see," The Chief said. "Where did you get the vehicle?"

"My grandmother gave it to me."

The man's eyes narrowed. "Are you sure?"

What was he suggesting? River shot a quick look at her wide-eyed friend, who raised her shoulders with a shrug.

River sat straighter. "Yes, I'm sure. I even have the title and registration in my backpack."

"Could I see those, please?"

"Yes, of course." Thank goodness she had put those in her backpack. River hurried to her bedroom, found the papers, and handed them to him.

He studied the documents for a moment, then gave them to Gabriel, who looked at the papers as one of his eyebrows raised.

Her heart hammering in her chest, River sat again on the couch. "Before I left town, I went to the website, registered everything, and sent in the papers. If there's a problem, maybe it hasn't gone through the system yet."

The Chief took in a deep breath before giving it a slow release. "Okay, I need some answers. The county picked up what was left of the car. Once the vehicle identification number, or VIN, was placed in the system, it was flagged as reported stolen."

"What?" Lila jumped to her feet. "It wasn't stolen. River's grandmother gave it to her."

He held up a hand. "Please let me continue."

Lila sat closer to River and gave her a look that said she was more angry than afraid.

The Chief continued. "I called the woman who reported the stolen vehicle."

River's stomach churned. It had to have been her mother. She probably planned on selling the car to use the money for a shopping spree. "What did she say?"

"She was agitated to learn it had been destroyed. She also asked where it had been found and if there was a body inside."

River sucked in a breath. Had her mother been worried that she had been killed? Probably not. Knowing her, she wanted River to be dead.

Lila rubbed River's back and addressed the officer. "I bet she was even more upset when you told her there wasn't a body."

The Chief averted his gaze. "I'd rather not say."

Lila opened her mouth, closed it, and blew out a breath. "I bet she didn't even ask if anyone was alive and with the car, did she?"

He shook his head. "No."

River rocked back and forth. She knew her parents didn't love her, but did they hope she was dead?. Why hadn't she taken her grandmother and ran away sooner? If only Nana hadn't been too frail to travel. River swallowed hard, trying to tamp down the emotion threatening to escape.

Lila growled. "That shows you what a miserable excuse for a mother that River has. Did you tell her where the car was found?"

"Yes."

Stifling a sob ballooning in her throat, River raked her hands through her hair. She didn't want her parents to know where she was. What if they showed up here? Where would she go?

"River." The Chief moved closer and leaned down to get her attention. "I told her where the car had been towed, which is close to the joint military base and almost an hour from here. I did not tell her where the car was originally found or that you were in Crawdad Beach."

River put her hand over her mouth to cover her trembling lip. "Thank you."

Gabriel returned the documents. "Keep these in a safe place. We don't know everything that has happened with you and your situation, but we'll keep watch for anyone who might harm you."

Why would they care about her? "Thank you." Trying not to have a full-out cry, River walked them to the door.

The Chief stopped and handed her his card with the police station and their cell numbers. "Don't hesitate to call if you need us."

Unable to speak, River nodded and closed the door.

Chapter 10

Her mother had reported the car stolen and then asked if there were bodies inside.

River slumped against the closed door. Her mother hadn't asked if River had been found or even if she was okay because she didn't care. Her mother never cared. She was upset she didn't get the car to sell and hoped River had died in the fire.

Lila hugged her. "I'm sorry."

In the comfort of her friend's arms, River's tears broke free. She couldn't cry around her parents. Her mother would slap her face if she did.

All her life, River felt like she wasn't wanted. Now she knew it was true. Why was she even born, and why did her parents adopt her? Her dad barely tolerated her, and her mother used her like slave labor. Her only fond memories were her grandmother, Lila, and a few school friends.

River swallowed hard. There was nothing for her in Texas. She had to start over and leave everything behind. That was it. She could be a new person here. No one knew her. She didn't have to tell anyone about her past. She'd just leave it behind and start fresh.

"Come back with me, please." Lila squeezed her tighter.

River squirmed out of the embrace and swiped the tears from her face. "No. What if this is where I get a new life? What if God brought me here? You and your parents know the truth about me and how I was raised. These people don't know anything. I can pretend everything was okay."

Lila scrunched up her nose. "I don't know about that. Even the police realize your mother isn't good."

"They don't have to know everything."

"But, if you keep walls around your past, how can you move into a new future?"

River huffed. "I knew I should have changed my name."

"Taking on a different name doesn't change you."

"Maybe not, but starting now, I'm a new person. I'm going to work at the restaurant and leave my crappy life behind."

"Please don't leave me behind."

"I won't, but you don't have to tell anyone anything, okay? You can update your parents but don't tell anyone here anything. And if my sorry-excuse-for-parents call you, do *not* tell them where I am." This was the first time she had been free, and there was no way she would ever go back.

"Okay." Lila held up her hands. "I won't say anything., but promise you won't shut me out."

"Don't worry. You're my friend for life. I need to do this, start over. This is my chance."

"Alright, but I'm just a phone call away if you want to talk or need me to fly to see you."

"Thanks. I'll be okay."

Lila's expression said she wasn't so sure.

River straightened her back and pasted on a smile. "Since you don't have to leave until tomorrow afternoon, why don't we go to the beach?" She'd only been to the ocean a few times in her life. The best time was when she was ten when Lila's family took her with them on their vacation to Florida. The other two times, River's parents took her as a babysitter to watch the children of the other adults. Since the kids were only babies and toddlers, River had been stuck inside the whole time.

Lila grinned. "Okay, we can do that. I didn't bring a bathing suit, but we could eat dinner, drive around, or walk by the ocean."

"Let's do it. I'm going to embrace the town, the area, and my new life."

Monday morning came before she knew it. The time she had with Lila over the weekend had been great, plus when she came home the other night, there had been a huge basket full of goodies welcoming her to Crawdad Beach.

Now, she needed to make a new start. River put on her best jeans and her nicest T-shirt. She wasn't sure what to wear to work, but her options were limited. Her mother only bought River what was on a sale rack or at garage sales.

Today was a new day, and she needed to let go of her past. Shaking off the negative thoughts, she stepped outside her apartment, locked the door, and made her way downtown.

Once she arrived, since it was too early for the restaurant to open, River knocked on the glass door and waited.

"Good morning." Faith Hollis grinned as she let her inside. "Are you ready to get started?"

"I hope so."

Faith motioned for her to follow her to the kitchen and introduced her to the other staff. The first cook, Boone, a middle-aged man, bobbed his bald head in greeting. Kurt, who looked close to her age, grinned and waved a spatula in welcome.

"Glad you're joining us," Ursula, the other waitress, said.

Everyone was wearing short-sleeve polo shirts with an embroidered cartoon crawdad wearing a chef's hat on the pocket. The guys wore blue shirts with peach trim, and the women's shirts were peach colored with a blue trim.

Faith handed River a shirt. "I think I got your size correct, and I washed it for you so it would be nice and soft for your first day."

She bit her lip to stop it from trembling. The shirt would be one of the few new things she'd ever gotten. "Thank you."

"You can change in the restroom, and there are lockers in the office where you can place your valuables. You'll shadow Ursula this morning, and she'll teach you anything you need to know about being a waitress."

"Thank you. I will try my best."

Faith patted River's arm. "I'm sure you will do fine."

Once she got ready, she found Ursula waiting for her.

Ursula had brown hair and brown eyes and looked close to her age. "I'm glad you will be here to help. The days are enjoyable but busy. I'm sure Faith told you a few things already about what they expect."

"No, she didn't tell me anything." River leaned toward her and kept her voice quiet. "I've never done this before. I don't know anything."

"No problem. Ask any questions you might have. Okay? Nobody will make you do this alone until you're ready."

River nodded, but now that she was standing here, she wasn't sure she could handle being a waitress. Maybe she should ask to work in the kitchen away from people.

Ursula handed River a black pad and pen. "This is where you write down the order to take to the kitchen. You don't have to take customers money. Faith and George take care of that for us. Since people seat themselves, you'll have to pay attention as they arrive and ensure no one sits too long before they get service."

She handed River a menu. "Take one of these home with you tonight to get familiar with what we offer. Most of the regular dishes are numbered, which makes it easier to take the orders. If anyone gives you a hard time, tell Faith or George, and they'll handle the situation. But don't worry, that doesn't happen very often."

Feeling lightheaded, River grabbed the side of a table. "I don't know that I can do this."

Ursula moved closer and whispered in her ear. "Have you ever had a job before?"

"No." She didn't want to tell her she hadn't even visited many restaurants.

"Don't worry. It's going to be okay. We all have to start somewhere. Just follow me around, and I'll take care of you."

At opening time, Faith unlocked the doors, and what looked like a thousand people rushed inside and sat at the tables. Trying not to hyperventilate, River followed Ursula as they took orders.

By the time the day ended, her feet and head were throbbing. How on earth could she be a waitress? She couldn't remember half of what Ursula had told her, and even though most of the customers were friendly, it was all so overwhelming.

River tried not to cry. Maybe she could ask to be a dishwasher or help cook? Why did she think she could find a job? She should have gone with Lila and lived with her family. River changed back into her T-shirt and unlocked the locker where she'd placed her purse.

"You did a great job today." Faith stood in the doorway.

"I didn't do anything, really." River stared at the tile floor.

Faith came next to her and took her hands in hers. "River, I offered you a job so you can succeed. No one will push you to do anything until you're ready." She squeezed her hands. "Ursula told me you hadn't worked before."

Moisture building in her eyes, River sniffled. "I don't know that I can do this."

"Sure, you can. I have no doubt you are an intelligent young woman who can be successful with whatever task you are given." Faith released her hands, and the plump woman pulled River into a soft, comforting embrace and held her close. "It's going to be okay. We will work with you to find your perfect spot."

Not sure how to react, River stood stiff but then let herself relax and put her arms around the woman.

River squeezed her eyes shut to try and stop her tears. Besides hugs from Lila or her grandmother, any affection had been extremely rare.

Enjoying the moment, River relaxed against Faith's soft body.

Chapter 11

Hands trembling, River couldn't believe she had her very first paycheck. She'd made it a whole two weeks as a waitress and was an actual employee. Meeting new people had been more enjoyable than she could have imagined. Nana would be proud of her. River had even surprised herself with how well she'd done at the job. She'd memorized the menu and even knew the names of many of the customers.

Now, if River could save enough money, she could get a car and not need to walk or rely on others. Then again, she had to pay rent and utility bills. How much would that be? And what about automobile insurance costs, groceries, and stuff like that?

Maybe she should have accepted the offer to live with Faith or Maybelline. River shook her head. No. She was going to make it on her own. She had to.

Staring at the check, she paused. What could she do with a check? She didn't have a bank account, and there wasn't even a branch nearby, only an ATM. Could her parents trace her if she opened an account in her name? Not that they probably would want to find her, but she didn't want to take a chance.

"Do you need a ride to the bank?" Faith asked from where she was sitting at her office desk.

"I'm not sure. I guess so, but I don't have an account anywhere." At least not here. The one in Texas had been in her name, but no amount would be safe with her mother on the signature card.

"That's right. I didn't think about that since you're new to the area. Plus, you don't have a car. Would you like us to pick you up next Sunday for church?"

"I guess so." River shrugged. "But I don't have anything nice to wear." She mainly had jeans and casual shirts.

"Not to worry. I have an idea about that. For now, do you need anything from the grocery store?"

River didn't want to admit the only food she'd eaten the last week was the restaurant's meals provided for employees. "I don't want to trouble you."

"You are never a problem," Faith smiled. "Let me finish up, and I'll drive you over."

"Thank you." She'd only buy what she needed since she still didn't know how much rent she'd have to pay. Thank goodness, the Bowmans, or whoever had the duplex before her, had left dishwashing liquid, washing machine soap, dryer sheets, and even shampoo and body wash.

"I'll take care of any additional funds you might need." Faith stacked papers on her desk. "Tomorrow morning around ten, when things get a little quieter, I'll drive you to a bank so you can set up an account. And I would love to shop for you and get you some new clothes."

River shook her head. "I don't have much money." She didn't want to waste a penny since she wasn't sure how long her funds would last.

"Please let it be my treat. My daughter lives in another state, and I have missed shopping for her. And with your cute little figure, finding you some new clothes will be fun."

"I'll pay you back."

Faith waved a dismissive hand. "Don't you give that another thought. Getting to shop with you will be a blessing for me."

River tried not to get emotional. She couldn't imagine shopping for new clothes. "I don't know what to say."

"No words necessary. I'm looking forward to it."

"Thank you so much." Fighting tears at how sweet Faith was being, River bit her lip as she considered asking about the name situation.

"Is something else troubling you?" Faith tilted her head and gave her a concerned look.

"Would it be possible to change the name on the check to Andrea Sawyer? That's my middle name."

Faith patted the chair next to her. "Let's have a little chat."

Although unsure what she might say, River did as asked. Crossing her legs, she tried not to act as nervous as she felt.

"I can reissue another check for you," Faith said. "However, would you be willing to tell me why you're worried about using your first name?"

"I thought it would be a little safer."

Faith didn't say anything for a moment. "River, is someone after you?"

Not expecting a direct question like that, River stared at the floor. "I don't know. I don't want to be found."

"Sweet girl, I'm so sorry for whatever you've been through. We can talk to a banker tomorrow and ask what would be best. And you probably need to get a new driver's license from our state. We'll have to look into what we need to do for that."

Thank goodness her mother had let her get a license when she turned sixteen. River never had her own car, but her mother sometimes let her drive Nana's car to the grocery store or take Nana to the doctor.

Faith patted her arm. "I'll call Maybelline and Chester to cover for us so we can take extra time to get everything taken care of for you."

"You would do that, and they would do that too?"

"Of course. Crawdadians are big on helping one another. Plus, when Chester is here working, it's always entertaining. George will be thrilled since they're buddies." Faith chuckled.

"Thank you, this is very nice of you all. I need to start paying rent, too. I appreciate Julie letting me stay over there."

"She said you have been the perfect tenant." Faith smiled as she stood and took her purse from her desk drawer. "Let's get you groceries. I need to pick up a few items for me and George anyway." Faith pulled her into a hug. "You're part of the family now, so don't hesitate to let us know what you need." With a gentle motion, Faith swayed as she hugged and patted River's back.

Laughter came from the kitchen, and Faith gave River another pat and gently stepped out of the embrace. "I'll grab some cash and let George know where we're going. I'll meet you in the back parking lot."

Leaning against the brick building, River wiped tears as she waited outside the back door. How could Faith and so many people be kind to her? Nana would have told her God was watching over her. River glanced up at the sky. She sure hoped so because her first eighteen years had been a nightmare.

Sammie stopped his shopping cart on the cereal aisle at Mitchell's grocery store and stared at all the sugar-filled, carbohydrate-heavy choices. His parents would cringe at his lack of healthy eating, but cooking for one person wasn't worth the effort.

He did miss his mom's farm-to-table meals. At least she gave him a good supply of leftovers when he ate at his parent's house every Sunday after church. His mom would make him a plate anytime he stopped by their place, but he wanted to make it on his own. Besides his house, he had nine acres of land. Maybe someday, he could build a life with a wife and family in town or on his property.

Sammie chose one of the blander cereals that seemed somewhat healthier than the rest and placed it in his cart. Maybe he could get up earlier and start eating breakfast at Tiddlywinks. The meal choices would be healthier, and he'd get to see River. She might not know he was alive, but he would enjoy watching her work. Well, not so much the work thing. He'd enjoy watching her.

Did that make him a stalker? No, surely not. Sammie rubbed the back of his neck. He liked River, and she was really pretty, but would she even date a guy like him?

He was twenty-one, but some people saw him as a kid. He'd worked since he could walk, enjoyed staying busy, and loved what others called a simple life. He might still be young, but he was a man. He had a job, a house, a pickup truck, and even had money saved. Yet, he was a small-town guy, and most women seemed to want someone more successful and ambitious.

Sammie did have ambitions. He took online college courses at night and already had a two-year business degree. God willing, he'd move up to manage Doohickeys someday so he could stay in Crawdad Beach.

Would he even have a chance with someone as gorgeous as River? He didn't know much about her, but maybe he could ask her out. Then again, he probably wasn't good-looking or successful enough for someone like her.

Sammie pushed his cart around the corner to the next aisle. Screeching to a stop, he gulped in air. He'd almost hit River. Her blue-grey eyes stared at him like he was from outer space.

He knew it. He never had a shot with someone like River.

Backing up, he waved an apology and ran for cover.

Chapter 12

What was that about?

Standing in the aisle, River checked her clothes. Why would Sammie look at her and then run? Was something wrong with her?

A soft chuckle came from behind River. "I think Sammie has a crush on you," Faith said with a mischievous grin.

"Me?"

"You have no idea what a beautiful girl you are, do you?"

Heat rose up River's back. *Beautiful?* How could that be? Her mother always told her she was ugly and plain. "You're just being nice."

"No, sweet girl. You are a beautiful young woman, and I believe you also have a beautiful heart."

Her eyes moist, River pretended to study items on the shelf. Why would someone as cute as Sammie want anything to do with her? She was a stranger in town, and he didn't even know who she was. Then again, maybe that would work in her favor because who would ever want to date her? Even her parents didn't want her.

River pushed the cart and picked up her pace. She needed to get back to her place. She didn't want Faith to have to wait on her. Grabbing a few essentials, River turned toward the checkout counters.

Faith's gaze flicked to the grocery cart and then to River. "Is that all you're going to buy?"

"I don't need much." She couldn't afford more than what was necessary since she still hadn't talked to Julie about how much her rent would be. What if she wanted more than she could afford?

"You need to put some meat on your little bones."

River shrugged and stepped up to the checkout counter. "I'll be fine."

"Well, you need to keep eating at the restaurant because as little as you have in your cart, you will starve."

"Starve?" River grinned as she laid her items on the conveyor belt since the comment sounded like something her Nana would say.

"You know what I mean. You need to eat to stay healthy."

"Yes, ma'am."

Faith grinned as she shook a finger at her. "You need to eat meat. A big juicy steak and a salad. That's what you need."

River rolled her eyes. As though she could afford a big steak.

"I'll cook you a steak."

River turned toward the deep voice.

Sammie stood in line behind her. Being so close to him, she could see how much taller he was than her. His body lean but muscular, not too much, just right.

With a shy smile, he held up a package of meat. "I could cook you one this evening if you're available. I'll even make a salad." He gazed at her, then Faith, to the floor, and back to River. Obviously, he wasn't as confident as his words sounded.

Faith, smiling like crazy, clucked like a hen. "Oh, that would be so nice. Don't you agree, River?"

Sammie was asking her on a date? Or, like a date? At his place? Even if he was very cute, she didn't know him or where he lived.

His chocolate-brown eyes held her gaze. He swallowed hard. "I live a street over from you."

"You can trust him. I've known Sammie all his life," Faith said as her gaze bounced back and forth between them.

As though trying to help her indecision, River's stomach growled loud enough the entire store probably heard.

Sammie gave a soft chuckle. "I could pick you up in an hour if that would be okay. Don't worry about changing. You look great." His neck reddened, and he looked away momentarily before returning his gaze. "We can sit outside. I have a screened-in patio where I'll put the steaks on the grill."

River bit her lip as she tried to figure out what to do. She wanted to spend time with Sammie, but spending time with a guy was scary. Her stomach growled again. *Traitor*.

Sammie hoped his request sounded more confident than he felt. He couldn't believe he'd jumped in and asked her to come over for dinner. River's stomach was ready to eat, but from the look on her face, he wasn't sure she was brave enough to take up his offer. He probably should have waited to ask her to his place, but she was standing there, and he had bought steaks since they were on sale. He was pretty good with grilling and knew how to make a salad.

River took a deep breath and nodded. "Okay, I'll have dinner with you."

His smile was so wide he probably looked goofy, but he didn't care. "Thank you." He grabbed his cell from his back jeans pocket. "Can I text you my number?"

Her gaze was hesitant. "Okay. Since you only live on the next street, I'll just walk over."

"Sure, that'd be fine." She probably wanted to be able to leave his place whenever she could. Hopefully, she'd stay long enough for him to get to know her better.

As River turned back to checkout, Sammie looked in his basket. He thought he had everything he needed. His mom's leftovers on Sunday had included a nice salad. He could throw a couple of potatoes in the microwave, then put them on the grill to give them a smoky flavor. His mouth watered just thinking about it.

The checker stated the amount for River's groceries, and she started to put her credit card in the machine.

Faith laid her hand on River's arm. "Put that back in your purse. Let me get that for you."

River's cheeks turned pink. "That's not necessary."

"I know it isn't, but I want to bless you. Plus, you are barely buying enough food."

Since River looked embarrassed, Sammie pretended to study the candy display. Was she having money trouble? He knew how to help the widows in town, but what could he do with River that wouldn't seem like he was coming on to her?

Maybe he could talk to Faith and see what she suggested. Even better, he could ask River if she'd like some of the produce from his parent's farm.

River finished gathering her groceries and gave him a cute, shy grin before following Faith out the door.

Sammie couldn't believe River was coming over. He'd never dated anyone that beautiful. As soon as he finished checking out, he hurried home. He needed to take a quick shower, make sure the house was clean, and get everything ready to cook the meal.

Sammie prayed River would be comfortable and enjoy being with him. He also asked God to help him not say or do anything idiotic. He didn't want to get tongue-tied because River Sawyer was actually coming to his house.

Chapter 13

Sitting in a hammock chair suspended from Sammie's screened-in-patio ceiling, River pushed her feet on the slate patio to sway back and forth. Sammie sat beside her in a matching chair and kept in time with her movement.

River couldn't believe how comfortable she felt with him, almost like when she spent time with Nana or Lila. Dinner was great, and he'd kept the conversation moving forward, sharing about growing up in Crawdad Beach.

She turned her attention back to what he had just said. "You had a pet rabbit?"

Sammie's dimple showed with his smile. "Yes. Named him Reginald."

"Reginald, the rabbit?" She giggled at a visual of a proper-looking bunny like an English gentleman.

"Since my parents are farmers, they didn't appreciate Reginald sampling their produce, so I caught him and made him my pet. I did take him out for exercise every now and then, and that's when a coyote came after him."

River cringed. "Oh, no. Did Reginald get away?"

"Of course. I wouldn't bring up something like that without a happy ending. How about you? Did you have any pets?"

"Not really." River shook her head. "My parents didn't want anything in the house." Including her. The tomcat she'd befriended had to stay outside since her parents didn't want anything to mess up their house. Now that she thought about it, that was a ridiculous excuse since they had so many parties.

Sammie surveyed her for a moment. "Sorry about that. So, what would you get if you could get a pet now?"

She shrugged. "I don't know."

"I think you should get a dog. Something cute and cuddly but protective. My grandparents had a toy poodle named Brutus. His bowlegged back legs made him look like a little western cowpup. He even used to wear a little blue bandana around his neck."

"Brutus?" River snorted a giggle.

Grinning, Sammie nodded. "The dog thought he was tough, but he was a lover, not a fighter. However, if squirrels were in the yard, he would bark up a storm and then huff as they turned tail and ran." He tilted his head as he looked at her. "I could see you with a Brutus-type dog."

Something to cuddle would be nice. Maybe someday she would get a kitty or puppy. She didn't even have a stuffed animal.

A comfortable silence settled over them. In the evening breeze, a bird chirped in the trees. A squirrel dug at something in the grass, paused, looked their way, then ran behind some bushes.

"Are you enjoying living in Crawdad Beach?" Sammie asked.

"I am. I like my job, and the people are nice." The work kept her busy, and she was getting to know the regulars. Even the town's visitors were usually friendly.

"Crawdad Beach has good people. It's not perfect, but most do care about one another. Did you like where you grew up?"

That wasn't a question River wanted to answer. She tried to act nonchalant. "The town was okay, I guess."

"So, what did you do for fun?"

"Fun?" She tried to think of something. "School was okay. I like to read. I enjoyed hanging out with my friend Lila or my grandmother."

"Is your grandmother back in Texas?"

"No, she passed away. That's why I left." River tried to ignore the ache pressing down on her chest. The week of her high school graduation, Nana had gripped River's hands and told her she wouldn't be there much longer, that she was going to a better place. She told River to leave and never return, to break their family's cycle and walk with Jesus wherever He led. Nana then had her caretaker, Zachariah, help River prepare her things.

River had clung to her grandmother and cried until she couldn't cry anymore, said a final goodbye, and left. Why didn't Nana let her stay until she passed? Why did she make River leave right then?

Sammie planted his feet to stop his chair from swaying, then gazed at her, his expression concerned, "I'm sorry, River. Did you live with her?"

River tried to steady her thoughts and tamp down her emotions. "She stayed with me in my room from the time I was thirteen." Nana's accident had been on River's birthday. She had come home from school, and as usual, there weren't any party or gifts. There never had been a celebration on her birthday. Nana showed up at the house, held by a man in medical scrubs. That night, Nana moved into River's room and stayed.

"You were her caregiver?"

"Kind of." Even though Nana could get around using a walker, she hadn't been mobile enough to drive or stay on her own. Zachariah would help three times a week. River didn't mind caring for her grandmother since Nana kept her company while her parents did their own thing.

"I'm sorry for your loss." Sammie's gentle voice and words washed over her, soothing some of her soul's soreness. But she would always miss Nana.

Sammie put his chair back in motion. River hadn't shared much, but enough to know she needed time to process. He couldn't imagine what it was like for her to lose her grandmother. He wished they had been friends long enough for him to hug or provide comfort.

Keeping his chair in motion in time with hers, he waited and prayed. After what seemed a long time, he checked his watch and noted it was almost nine. Would River need to get up early for work? Either way, he hoped she was ready to talk again. "Do you like the ocean?"

It took a moment before she glanced his way. "I do. I haven't been there many times."

Sammie couldn't hide his surprise. "You've only been a few times? I could take you, and we could swim or walk on the beach if you'd like that."

River bit her lip, then nodded. "That sounds fun, but I don't have a swimsuit. Maybe I can get one tomorrow when Faith drives me to the bank. She's also taking me clothes shopping."

"Faith is a nice woman. She's also an amazing prayer warrior. She's good friends with my mom since my family's farm provides fresh produce for the restaurant."

"I didn't know that. Your family owns Harvest Grace Farms?"

"Yep, that's us."

"I must have met your mom and dad then. They're nice. Maybelline mentioned that you're a descendant of the first settlers. That's very cool."

Sammie sat a little taller and puffed out his chest. "I am proud to be a true native Crawdadian."

That comment got her to smile.

"I better get home." She rose to her feet. "Thank you for a wonderful dinner and a really nice evening."

He stood next to her. "Thank you for coming over. It's been great." He followed her to the door. "I'll walk you home."

"That's not necessary."

"It might not be necessary, but as a Crawdadian gentleman, I must see that you are given a proper escort to your abode." He did a little bow.

She gave a soft chuckle. "How could I refuse?"

Sammie offered her his arm. River looked confused for a moment, hesitated, then slid her hand into the crook of his elbow.

Loving the feel of her soft fingers on his arm, he chatted about the people who lived in the houses along the road as they made the way back to River's place.

When they arrived, she released the hold on his arm and stepped closer to the door. "I had a very nice time."

"I did, too. Thanks again for coming over. Maybe we can head to the beach next weekend."

"I'd like that."

He smiled at her sweet expression. "Good. It's a date."

River returned his smile, unlocked her door, and hurried inside.

As much as he would have loved to kiss her, he would take his time and not rush. She probably needed a friend more than anything else, and if God answered his prayers, someday they would have more than a friendship.

Chapter 14

River closed her door and happily sank on her couch. The evening with Sammie had been wonderful. He made her feel comfortable whether they were talking or just sitting together.

Although his house was under renovation, it had been clean and well-kept. Home improvement shows were always fun to watch, so maybe he would let her help him paint or work on a project.

Sammie had even talked about his faith, which was nice. And he didn't come on to her or even act like he wanted anything but to be her friend. Maybe he wasn't attracted to her. She groaned. She couldn't blame him. What did she have to offer?

River checked the time. Even though it was nine-thirty at night, she needed to find out about the rent. Based on her first paycheck with taxes already removed, she now had an idea of what she could afford each month. With her tips, she might be able to go even higher. That would leave her enough for groceries and anything else she might need. But if she had to pay utilities and Wi-Fi, what would that leave her? Plus, she needed to give her cheap phone more minutes, which would take more money.

She hadn't thought about healthcare until Faith mentioned the restaurant helped their employees with basic healthcare. Faith also had given her a company to contact if River needed dental insurance.

River took a deep breath and went next door, ready to face whatever came next.

Fifteen minutes later, she returned and wanted to jump for joy. Julie told her that someone in town had already paid for River's first month, and then she told her how much the rent would be afterward. Thankfully, it wasn't as much as she had thought. How could they afford to charge her that little for a furnished, lovely duplex apartment?

River knew it wasn't luck. God had given her another blessing. She could stay in Crawdad Beach and start saving for a car. Maybe she'd buy a bike or a scooter.

Before she let her thoughts run all over the place, she needed to thank God because her life was finally looking up.

The next morning, River grinned at Chester sitting at a restaurant table. "Where's Maybelline?"

"She's working at the library today, so I'm on my own. Which means I can have the big breakfast. Three eggs, two slices of bacon, two sausage patties, grits, hashbrowns, and biscuits."

River chuckled at his choice of what the staff privately called the heart attack platter. "I'll be back as soon as it's ready."

"I'll be waiting with bated breath," Chester said, then held up his hand. "Wait, I'm not sure what that means. The word doesn't mean like baiting a hook, does it?"

River choked back a laugh. "I have no clue."

Movement at the door turned her attention. Sammie smiled and waved as he took a seat.

She hurried to his table. "Good morning." She leaned closer. "Thank you again for a very nice evening."

"I had a great time. I'm looking forward to our beach trip."

"Me too." Heat rising to her cheeks, she stood straighter and tried to act more professional.

After she wrote down what Sammie wanted, she walked to the kitchen and gave the cooks her orders.

Ursula shimmied her eyebrows. "Looks like a romance is blooming."

Romance? River gulped.

"Ms. River, you have a fella?" Boone flipped pancakes as he looked her way.

"No, not really." River shook her head. "We're just friends."

"Just friends?" Ursula grinned. "The way you two look at each other I'd say there is more attraction than a simple friendship."

"So, who is the young man?" Boone asked.

"Sammie," Ursula said as she waltzed out of the kitchen.

"He's a good boy, Ms. River," Boone said. "I've known him all his life. He will treat you right."

Heat scorching her cheeks, River nodded and rushed out of the kitchen. Sammie was a friend, but she wouldn't mind having a boyfriend. Did he look at her as if he liked her? Not just like her, but like, liked her?

She peeked around the corner to where he was sitting. He really was cute. Trying to calm herself and her wayward thoughts, River grabbed a coffee pot and went to see if anyone needed a refill.

A man dressed in a business suit caught her attention and held up his cup.

She walked to his table and gave him a refill. "Is there anything else I can get you?"

His dark eyes grazed over her body. "You must have read my mind. I can think of many things I'd like you to give me. What time do you get off today?"

River shook her head. There was no way she would have anything to do with him. The man's slimy grin reminded her of some of her dad's party friends. River stepped back and bumped against someone.

"Sweetheart, is he giving you trouble?" Chester put his arm on her shoulder, steadying her. He lasered a look at the man. "You need to leave. *Now*. We don't take kindly to anyone harassing our women."

The guy smirked. "Sure, pops. As though you could do anything about it."

The next thing River knew, the guy was on his back on the floor, and Chester was scowling down at him. "I said it's time for you to go."

River gulped. How did Chester make a ninja move like that?

Sammie shot to his feet, sprinted over, and stood in front of River. His broad shoulders providing protection.

Scowling at Chester, the man brushed off his suit and threw cash on the table. "I won't be coming back here."

Sammie got in the man's face. "I think that would be wise. Go, and don't *ever* come back."

Both men escorted the jerk out the door as applause broke out in the restaurant.

Wide-eyed, Faith rushed toward River. "Is everything okay?"

She felt like she was in a daze. "Just a rude customer, but Chester and Sammie took care of him."

Sammie hurried back to her. His eyes softened as he rubbed River's arm. "Are you okay?"

Although she wished she could lean against him, she nodded. "Sure. I'm good." She glanced at her protectors. "Thank you both."

"Our pleasure," Chester said. He turned his gaze to Faith. "I hope you don't mind, but there was *no* way I wanted a man like that in your fine establishment harassing your wonderful employees."

"I completely agree." Faith gave a stern nod. "You are always welcome to be our restaurant bouncer."

Chester chuckled and slapped Sammie on the back. "Well, son, it looks like we have another employment opportunity."

Sammie did a slight bow toward River. "I'm happy to be at your service."

"Thank you, kind sir."

From across the restaurant, Ursula acted like she was swooning.

Fighting a grin, River turned to see if anyone else needed coffee. She'd never had anyone come to her rescue like Chester and Sammie.

She stopped by a table and refilled a man's cup who reminded her of an older version of Sean Connery. He looked up at her, his gaze intense but friendly. "My name's Wilder Templeton, this is my wife, Stella, and our friend, Mia." The ladies smiled as the man handed her a business card. "We're involved in security. Don't hesitate to call if you ever need help."

River thanked them and put the card in her jeans pocket. As she walked away, she wondered if they were the people the lady and her daughter had been discussing that day when she was in the bakery. Was the green-eyed lady named Stella the spy?

Between Chester's impressive moves, Sammie wanting to protect her, security people, and possible spies, Crawdad Beach had to be the best place ever.

Sammie paid for his meal, said goodbye to River, and stepped out onto the sidewalk. He wanted to make sure the guy who harassed her wasn't anywhere in town.

Chester followed him out the door. "You don't see him, do you?"

"No. I think he's gone."

"He better be. I wonder why he was here. We don't get many businessmen in town early in the morning."

"I was thinking the same thing. It's usually locals for breakfast and maybe a few visitors."

"The guy had been staring at River for a while."

Sammie's pulse notched up as he turned to Chester. "You don't think he was looking for her, do you?"

"I don't know. Since we aren't sure what, or who, River was running from when she came our way, I'm going to talk to Chief and Gabriel and give them a heads-up." Chester jogged down the street.

Sammie looked in the restaurant window to make sure River was still okay. He still had a few minutes to spare before he needed to get to work.

Breaking into a run, he passed through the downtown area to ensure the jerk guy wasn't still in town.

It looked like he'd left, but still, Sammie sent up a prayer for River's protection.

Chapter 15

How did she get so lucky? River corrected her thought. She wasn't lucky, she was blessed. After being protected from the man at the restaurant, Faith had taken River to the bank, and the kind banker let her use her middle name to set up the account. She didn't think her parents would try to track her, but it did make River feel safer.

She grinned as she laid her new clothes on her bed. Faith had taken her shopping and out to lunch. River tried to buy her clothes on sale, but Faith wouldn't let her and insisted on purchasing everything. River now had some of the cutest dresses she'd ever seen, new shoes, new tops and jeans, cute purses, and even new undergarments.

Now that she had dresses, she could feel comfortable attending church on Sunday. River nibbled on her fingernail. Faith had spent a lot of money and time. Even though she didn't want River to pay her back, she felt bad that anyone would spend money on her. She didn't deserve anything.

River shook off her negative thoughts. She needed to enjoy the gifts God had given her. She had a new place to live, a good job, and people who seemed to care about her.

Since it was already four thirty in the afternoon, she had the rest of the day off. Maybe she'd stop in and see

Sammie, then walk the trail next to the river. River put on one of her new casual outfits and headed out.

When she arrived on Main Street, she paused, peeked in the window at Knick Knacks, and waved at Grace and Jeremy. River grinned as they smiled and waved back. It felt so good to know people and be a part of the town.

Going further down the sidewalk, she stepped inside Doohickeys. The place was busy with customers. She didn't see Sammie, so she took her time exploring. The well-worn wood floors creaked as she wandered through the aisles. River grinned at a big wooden box marked whatchamacallits, then stopped to admire a display of old farm and house implements hanging on the back wall.

"Looking for something?"

River turned and smiled as Sammie walked toward her. "Not anymore."

His brows skyrocketed. "You're looking for me?"

"Yes. Faith let me off early today, and I thought I'd drop by and say hello."

Sammie's smile widened. "Hello."

"Thank you again for coming to my rescue this morning."

"My pleasure. I'm sorry the guy was such a jerk."

"I guess I need to expect it sometimes."

"I hope not." Sammie stepped closer. "I've been praying for your protection."

"Aw, thank you. That's really sweet." River's cheeks heated again. What was it about being around him that made her body do that? It wasn't like she hadn't liked guys before. But since her parents had expected her home to take care of Nana, River had squelched most of her guy thoughts. With Sammie, she had thought a lot about him.

His dimple showed with his grin. "What are you doing with the rest of your evening?"

"I was going to go to the park, walk on the trail, and then hang out at home."

"Want some company? I get off in about fifteen minutes."

"I'd like that very much."

"Good. Great. Let me take care of a few things, and I'll be right back with you."

River grinned as she watched him hurry away. She hadn't thought about him joining her this evening, but she was thrilled he was. She continued walking around the store, looking at all the items. Some she knew what they were, but many of them she had no clue.

"Ready to go?" Sammie came toward her. "Eric said I could go ahead and leave. He and Gloria will be able to handle any last-minute customers."

When they arrived at the town park, River grinned as they passed Crepe Myrtles in full bloom. A gust of wind carried a shower of pink flowers around them as they made their way to the trail. Sunshine filtered through the trees, providing relief from the warm afternoon.

"Besides this morning, did you have a good day?" Sammie asked.

"I did. Faith took me to the bank to set up my account, then she took me shopping, and I got new clothes."

Sammie grinned as he glanced her way. "I like your outfit. You look really nice."

"Thanks. I've never had new stuff like this."

"You haven't?"

"No, My parents didn't like spending money on me."

Sammie stopped. "I'm sorry, River. That stinks."

"It's okay." She didn't want to go down that depressing hole and ruin her evening. "How about you? Did you have a nice day?"

"Yeah, we stayed really busy, so time flew. I was surprised it was almost closing time when you came in. Thanks for the invite to join you."

"I'm glad you were available."

They continued walking, and River's hand occasionally brushed against his, sending little happy zings up her arm. She'd always wondered about some of the descriptions in romance books she'd read. Nana only let her read Christian fiction, so there was never anything too graphic, but River wondered what an author meant about a man's voice getting husky. Her dad's voice usually sounded upset, or he didn't say much, at least not to her.

She also had read about women thinking about their heart pounding, lungs tightening, and knees buckling when they were around men they liked. She did notice some body changes when she was with Sammie. Her cheeks felt hot more often, and walking beside him did make her happy.

"Want to sit down?" Sammie pointed to a bench facing the river.

"Sure." She followed his lead.

He waited until she sat down before sitting next to her, then stretched his legs out in front of him. "I love coming here."

"It is really nice." River leaned back on the bench and watched the water in the small river shimmer in the light.

"I sometimes bring my lunch and sit here while I eat. Nature is calming. It's amazing all the variety of plants that God made. One of the cool things about growing up on a farm is seeing how tiny seeds can become a stalk of corn, a cucumber, squash, tomato, an eggplant, or a watermelon."

"That is neat. I guess I never thought about it. My mother would order stuff online and have it delivered to the house, so I didn't visit farms or even grocery stores that much."

"One day, I'll take you to my parent's farm and let you look around."

"I'd like that."

"My parents would gladly share some of their crops. Eating healthy like that is really good for you. We could go right now if you're up for it?"

River gulped. "Now?"

"Sure. My family doesn't bite. Plus, we might get there in time to eat dinner. My mom's cooking is the best."

"I've met your parents at Tiddlywinks, but barging in for a meal? Won't they be mad?"

"No. They love company."

"Really? My parents never wanted people to drop in on them unless they were having a party."

Sammie's gaze surveyed her for a moment as though he couldn't imagine that thought, then he stood and pulled her to her feet. "Then you are in for a treat." Not letting go of her hands, his gaze moved from her eyes to her lips.

River now understood when authors wrote about a heart leaping because her heart definitely had jumped in her chest. Or was that leaped? Either way, her heart was pitter-pattering, and her pulse skyrocketed.

He straightened and looked away. "I guess we better go."

She tried not to whimper, but still, it leaked out. She had hoped he would kiss her.

Sammie's head tilted. He grinned as his gaze searched hers. Wrapping his arms around her, he pulled her close. His lips touched hers with tender, sweet kisses that made every thought in her head disappear, and her heart puddle into a happy sigh.

Sammie hadn't intended to kiss River so soon, but when she whimpered, he couldn't help himself.

Well, he could have, but he didn't exactly have regrets. On the contrary, he'd never kissed anyone like he kissed River. Or should he say, he'd never been kissed by anyone like her. Whew! The kisses were incredible.

He held her close. Her heartbeat fast, her arms around him, River rested her head on his chest. Now that they had crossed the kissing stage, should he hold her hand when they left?

Sammie didn't know what he was supposed to do. As much as he enjoyed having River in his arms, how long should they stand here? Should he pull away first or let her take the lead?

Holding River as tenderly as he could, Sammie prayed for help.

Chapter 16

Could they stay like this forever? Safe in Sammie's arms, River sighed. *If only*.

Her parents were never affectionate. The few hugs her mother gave were when someone was watching, and her mother wanted to appear loving. At least River's grandmother had been a good hugger.

Sammie was probably already tired of her. Stepping away from his embrace, River crossed her arms over her chest. Best protect her heart while she could. Sammie would probably not want anything else to do with her since she was the one who first wanted to kiss.

"Hey." He tilted her chin up and smiled. "Thank you for the best kisses I've ever had."

"Really?"

His eyes tender, he chuckled. "Oh, yeah. That was great."

"You're not just saying that?"

"No, definitely not." He brushed a hand against her cheek. "You're wonderful."

Her lip trembling, River looked away and pushed back a tear threatening to escape. How could Sammie be so nice to her?

Sammie put his hands on her arms. "I don't know what you've been told or what you believe about yourself, but please believe me, you are beautiful and a great kisser.

He thought she was beautiful and a great kisser? River uncrossed her arms and smiled. Boy, did she want to kiss him again.

Sammie took her hands in his. "So, are you okay with going to my parent's house for dinner?"

All her happy emotions disintegrated. "I don't know."

"Don't worry. You'll love them, and they will love you." He brought their joined hands to his lips. "I'll tell them you are a great kisser."

Horrified at the thought, River stepped back. "No! You wouldn't tell them that, would you?"

Sammie chuckled. "Of course not." His gaze turned apologetic. "I'm sorry. I was teasing you. Please don't be upset."

River tried to catch her breath. He was teasing, not in a mean way like her parents used to do. Sammie wasn't like them, but would his family be sweet, too? His mom and dad had been nice when she met them at the restaurant, but how would they be at their own home?

"We don't have to go to if you're uncomfortable."

Part of her wanted to run away, but seeing where he grew up and how he was raised would be interesting. It would probably be terribly uncomfortable, but it would answer some questions about him. She could see how they all interacted with one another, and if she didn't like what she saw, she wouldn't ever have to go back.

She looked into his eyes and nodded. "Okay, I'll do it."

"You look like I'm taking you to get your teeth pulled. I promise if I see that you are not enjoying yourself, I will make a quick excuse, and we'll leave. Okay?"

"Okay." River nibbled on her lip. "Thank you."

"I'll send them a text so they can be expecting us." Sammie sent the message, then took River's hand and led her along the trail. "Mom likes to have the table set for whoever is coming. The more people enjoying her cooking, the better."

Having her hand in his, River's nerves settled as she kept in step with him. Maybe everything would be alright.

Sammie held River's hand as he showed her around the farm. Even though, at first, she'd been nervous, she'd settled in without problems, and the meal had gone well. His parents were great at making people comfortable, and his mom's cooking was out of this world. They were sensitive about asking River questions, keeping the conversations moving without awkward silences.

Her wide-eyed curiosity about the farm and animals reminded him of his little niece. River asked a zillion questions about the animals and what it was like for him growing up on the farm. Even walking with her through the fields was enjoyable.

Once they reached where the tree line started, he stopped and pointed toward his acreage. "Someday, I will probably build a house back here in the trees."

"You might live on your parent's farm?"

"Yes and no. My grandparents gifted ten acres for each of the grandkids. I own nine because I sold one acre to my brother so I could have money to buy a house in town to be closer to work. Crawdad Beach is where my family is from and where I want to stay. How about you? Do you have someplace you want to go?"

"Not really. I do like living here."

"Good. I hope you always do." Sammie tucked a stray hair behind her ear and leaned down to kiss her.

Her breath quivered, and a small moan escaped. He held her close and was careful to keep his kisses from growing along with the passion he was feeling.

Sammie groaned and stepped back. "I better get you home."

"Is everything okay?" River's hand rested on his chest. "Did I do something wrong?" She looked so hurt.

He ran a finger along the side of her cheek. "You didn't do anything wrong. I love being with you. I don't want things to go too far."

River blinked a few times as though she didn't understand, and then her face flamed red. "Oh." She wrapped her arms around herself and looked away.

Sammie rubbed the back of his neck. He'd been homeschooled until his last two years of high school; then, between school, working on the farm, and working at Doohickeys, he hadn't gotten too involved with anyone. As good as River kissed and as beautiful as she was, she probably had more practice than he did.

Would she think he was strange that he didn't have a string of ex-girlfriends? Or, maybe it wasn't that at all. From what he'd learned about River's past, it sounded like she had been pretty isolated. Still, he had a hard time thinking that she didn't have a ton of boyfriends.

"I guess you better take me home," River's voice was barely a whisper. She wouldn't even look at him as she walked away.

Sammie stifled a groan. What was he supposed to do now? He didn't want her to think he was upset with her or wasn't attracted to her, but how was he supposed to show or tell her that? Was praying for help with this kind of thing even a thing?

He caught up with her and waited until her blue-grey eyes, swimming in tears, looked his way. "River, I'm not upset with you. Not in any way. You're wonderful. It's that I'm ... well, I'm a..." He shook his head and raked his hand through his hair. "It's just I really like you, and I want to treat you like a lady." He breathed a sigh of relief and hoped she understood.

River swiped a tear from her cheek. "You like me?"

How did she not know how beautiful and wonderful she was? "I really like you."

The faintest smile touched her lips. "I really like you too."

Not wanting to waste the moment, Sammie cupped her face in his hands and gave River another kiss he hoped would convince her that he really, *really* liked her.

Rubbing her fingers across her lips, River lay in bed thinking about the wonderful afternoon and evening she had with Sammie. She couldn't believe he liked her. He was so cute and sweet, and his kisses were terrific.

Plus, it was incredible how comfortable she felt when she stepped into his parent's house, almost like their home gave her a warm hug. Could that be possible? Maybe it was because Sammie and his family were kind to one another and even kind to her. They talked about God and Jesus in a sweet, familiar, respectful way and told funny stories about the farm and animals.

What would it have been like to grow up with loving parents? She'd been in daycare as early as she could remember. Once old enough for school, she got ready by herself and rode the bus. Since the driver lived down the road, she was the first one on and the last one off.

Even as a kindergartener, she came home to an empty house. Her dad kept long hours, and when River's mom wasn't at work, she went shopping, partying, or to the spa to get beauty treatments. River sighed. At least Nana had loved her.

River rolled over, turned on her nightstand lamp, and picked up her Bible. In the front flap, she'd written verses to help her through her difficult days. The ones that stood out tonight reminded her that God takes care of the orphans, He's the God of all comfort, and even if our mothers forget us, God never does.

She flipped to Psalm 68:5 and read, *A Father to the fatherless, a defender of widows, is God in His holy dwelling.* Her gaze went to the following verse: *God sets the lonely in families and leads out the prisoners with singing.*

Chill bumps popped on her arms. Would God do that for her? Had he brought her to Crawdad Beach to give her a loving family? Could something good like that really happen to her?

Afraid to hope, she turned off the light.

Chapter 17

Throughout the night, River tried to pray, but her mind kept wandering. Her thoughts rambled like when a schoolteacher left the room, and the students would all talk at once.

River would start to pray, then off her brain would go, wishing her life had been different, replaying years of hurtful actions and comments her parents had made.

Why couldn't she have grown up in a nice family like Sammie? Then she felt guilty about complaining. So, she prayed for forgiveness. But then, she'd think of something else that hurt her, and her thoughts would run and whine down the poor me road.

When her alarm went off, River groaned. Faith and her husband, George, were taking her to church, which was nice. She just wished she'd gotten more sleep. River forced herself out of bed, showered, and got ready. She was nervous about going, but at least she had a new dress and shoes to wear. Not that nice clothes fixed anything, but if she were going to be nervous, she would at least look decent.

Thirty minutes later, when they arrived at the church building, Chester and Maybelline greeted her with hugs. Several other people also came over to welcome her. She already knew most of them since many were Tiddlywinks customers.

Faith and George led River to a pew, and she sat beside them.

"I'm glad you're here," Sammie said as he slid next to her.

Grateful to see him, River returned his smile. "Thanks. I'm a little nervous but excited to be able to come."

"I'll be glad to bring you next week."

"That would be nice." River hadn't thought that far in advance, but if he were offering, she would be happy to spend more time with him.

Music started, and everyone stood. Thank goodness, the words were on a big screen at the front so River could follow along. Sammie's voice was quiet but had such a nice tone that she leaned closer to hear him sing.

When the songs were over, everyone sat down, and River readied her Bible, hoping she could find any verses that might be used. Sammie also had a Bible, a journal he opened, and a pen ready to take notes. She hadn't thought about taking notes like at school.

Holding a group of brightly colored helium balloons, a man probably in his forties came and stood on the front stage. "Are you having trouble with your thoughts?"

River squirmed as the man seemed to look right at her.

"I understand," The pastor continued as he moved the balloons rapidly in front of his face. "The other night, I was tossing and turning in bed worrying about all sorts of worries when I realized that was a total waste of time. Instead of worrying, I should have corralled those thoughts and prayed."

He stopped the balloons from moving. "Second Corinthians 10:5 says we lead every thought away captive into the obedience of Christ. We don't take a thought, or those million thoughts, rattling around in our brains and try to hold them in our own strength. We prayerfully lead them away captive in the obedience and the power of Christ." The pastor released a balloon, and it floated away.

"Our circumstances may not change, but our thinking can," he continued. "Taking thoughts captive is retraining our brain and refocusing our focus. As believers, we're given the mind of Christ. We are *not* given the spirit of fear but are given power, love, and a sound mind. Therefore, we have the right, along with Christ's power, to deny access to thoughts that waste our time, that would cause us to stumble or pull away from God, or those that deprive us of sleep and soul rest."

River leaned forward, hoping she could remember what the preacher said. Since Sammie was taking notes, maybe he would let her look at them later.

"Therefore," the pastor continued, "when a thought comes to mind, ask yourself the following question. Is this thought honoring or pleasing to God? If not, get rid of it.

Don't let it linger in your mind." The pastor popped a balloon.

A few people jerked at the sound, and nervous laughter filled the room.

"The next question to ask is," the preacher continued, "will thinking this thought solve or help anything or anyone? Many are unhelpful, worthless mind-spinners. Lead those thoughts away captive in obedience to Christ. Pray and give them to God." He released another balloon.

"Last question. What does God's Word tell me about that thought? In John 8:32, Jesus said you will know the truth, and the truth will set you free. Read your Bible, know God's word, and if a thought doesn't align with scripture, move it out of your head." The pastor let another balloon go.

River hoped she could remember all he said. This was just what she needed.

The pastor paused a moment. "Thoughts also come when we need to forgive someone who wronged us. Jesus said, forgive, and you will be forgiven. Forgiving others blesses *us* with forgiveness. God knows what happened. He knows the truth and He promises justice for those who have been wronged. Grieve the pain, but don't let the past define your future, and don't allow what happened to you to be bigger than what Christ's sacrifice and grace has done for you. God is the God of all comfort. He heals the brokenhearted and binds their wounds. Nothing is impossible for God, and He will help you by His power forgive those who hurt you." The preacher let another balloon go.

"And, if you need help with forgiveness for yourself, go to God, repent, and remember He takes your sins and throws them as far as the East is from the West. Isaiah 44:22 reads I have swept away your offenses like a cloud, your sins like the morning mist. Return to me, for I have redeemed you." The pastor popped a balloon.

"When Christ is in you, you have His power to free you. You don't have to entertain every thought. When Jesus said to come to Him for rest, that means rest for everything. Whatever you are facing, whatever happened, whatever concerns you have, whatever causes you to fear or worry, take to Jesus. Turn the focus off of the thoughts and focus on our Savior and God.

"God, our Heavenly Father, loves you. So, release all your anxieties, worries, and concerns to Him. As Paul wrote in Philippians 4:6, be anxious for nothing, but in everything by prayer and supplication with thanksgiving, let your requests be made known to God. And the peace of God, which surpasses all comprehension, will guard your hearts and minds in Christ Jesus." The rest of the pastor's balloons floated to the ceiling.

"Philippians 4:8-9, finally, brothers and sisters, whatever is true, whatever is honorable, whatever is right, whatever is pure, whatever is lovely, whatever is commendable, if there is any excellence and if anything worthy of praise, think about these things and the God of peace will be with you."

The pastor continued sharing and closed in a prayer. After he finished, the people stood and sang another song.

River tried to sort through all the preacher had said. Did she have the right and power to take her thoughts captive? Was that even possible?

Maybe she could let go of some of the silly things she worried about. But releasing all the rotten things her parents had done to her was different. Forgive them? How could she?

God would have to understand that she had a right to be angry and hurt because her parents never deserved to be forgiven.

Chapter 18

Once the service ended, Sammie stood. River was looking down as though deep in thought. "Would you like to go to lunch?"

It took a moment before her gaze turned toward him. Maybe she was still thinking about the sermon. River shrugged. "Sure. That would be nice."

"Great." Sammie grinned at her, then turned to Faith and George, told them he would take River home, and then led her out of the church.

He opened the car door for her. "My parents said they'd love for you to join us."

River's shoulders dropped.

Uh oh. Had she thought he was asking her to go somewhere alone with him? Should he have done that instead of planning on taking her to his family's home? Maybe she was still thinking about the sermon.

On the ride to his parent's house, River remained quiet, her gaze out the side window.

"Did you enjoy the service?" Sammie asked.

She glanced his way and gave him what looked like a polite smile. "Yes, it was nice."

"I liked what the pastor said about releasing our thoughts."

"Yeah, that was good. I like what he said about that, but forgiving others is different." Her last comment came out as a whisper.

"That's a harder one, isn't it?" Sammie wanted to reach over and touch her but kept his hands on the wheel. He understood that problem.

"Your pastor doesn't know what people have been through, and saying we need to forgive and let it go is unfair." River's lip trembled. She turned away and crossed her arms over her chest.

He hadn't expected that reaction. Sammie pulled his pickup to the side of the road. "I'm sorry for whatever happened."

"It's not your fault." She didn't look at him.

"Forgiving others is a tough one. To be honest, I wouldn't even think about doing it, except that Jesus said that if we don't forgive others, we won't be forgiven."

River shot him a glare. "Are you sure he said that?"

Sammie prayed for help so that he wouldn't mess this up. "Yes, it's recorded in Matthew that Jesus said if we forgive other people for their sins, God will also forgive us, but if we don't forgive others, God will not forgive our sins."

"That's not fair."

"I agree it doesn't sound fair, but because God forgave us for everything we did, we need to do the same."

"That stinks. I mean, not the part about God forgiving us, but forgiving others. Why do we have to do that? That's not right. I'm not going to let them off the hook that easy."

"Forgiving someone else doesn't let them off the hook with God, but it lets you off the hook. It frees you." Hoping he could word things right, Sammie took a deep breath and prayed for help. "When I was a teenager, my dad took me deep-sea fishing, and I hooked the biggest swordfish you can imagine. I was strapped into a chair and kept reeling the fish in, and it would fight, and I'd keep reeling it in. My dad kept yelling at me to let it go and was even fighting with me over the road. But there was no way I was going to let that fish get away."

He waited to finish his story until River turned toward him, her gaze curious.

"I didn't realize the old chair I was in was pulling loose from the boat's deck," Sammie continued. "The harder that fish fought, the more I tugged on the reel, the more the chair was releasing. The next thing I knew, I was pulled out of the boat, chair and all."

River's eyes went wide. "Oh, no!"

"Thankfully, I was wearing a life vest, but until I released the rod, I was being pulled under. Once I let go, I could keep my head above the water. My dad and another one of his friends jumped in and helped get me to safety."

"I'm so glad you were okay." River gazed at him and then sighed as she rubbed her forehead. "Sammie, I feel like I've been pulled under most of my life. How can I forgive? Her voice was only a whisper.

He laid his hand on her arm. "I understand how hard it is, but until you do, it only keeps you under. Releasing the fish released me. So, when we forgive others, it releases us and lets us be forgiven."

Her eyes were watery when she looked at him. "I don't know." She turned away again.

"Would it be okay if I texted my parents and told them we'll come over another time? If you're up for company, we can do something else."

"Sure," River sniffled, "but I don't want your parents to think I don't like them. They're sweet people."

"They will understand." Sammie sent a quick message to his mom, explaining they would come over another time. Right now, he didn't want River to be alone. "I could drive through a fast food place, get us something to eat, and then we could go to the beach."

She didn't say anything for a moment; she just kept staring out the side window. "I guess, but I'm not dressed for that."

"How about I swing by your place to let you change? I keep casual stuff in my gym bag in case I need to help my parents on the farm after work."

River's gaze flicked his way before turning to face the window. "Okay."

At least she was still open to being around him. Sammie sent up another prayer for help.

River squeezed her arms tighter around herself. She needed to calm down. Church and seeing people she knew had been nice, plus she was with Sammie, had a new life, and was away from her parents. She should be happy. But all she could think about was having to forgive them. Ugh. They didn't deserve forgiveness. She probably didn't either, but that was different. Wasn't it?

God was big enough to forgive stuff, and she was just a person. The more time she spent in Crawdad Beach, the more she saw loving families with moms and dads who seemed to like being around their children. River stifled a groan. She would never understand why her parents had adopted her.

A speeding car zipped past them. Sammie yanked the steering wheel to keep his truck from getting hit. River cringed, waiting for a string of curse words, but Sammie kept driving as though nothing had happened. Her dad would have been screaming and cursing for thirty minutes.

When they arrived at River's apartment, Sammie grabbed his gym bag, hurried to her side of the truck to let her out, then followed her inside.

As they stepped inside, Sammie glanced around. "Nice place."

"Thanks. I can't take credit for how it looks, but I am grateful to be here."

"I'm glad you're here."

At his sweet smile, heat rose to her cheeks. She pointed toward the hallway. "You can change in the bathroom."

Sammie took his bag and closed the door behind him.

River hurried to her room to find something to wear. Since Faith had bought her a swimsuit, River's stomach fluttered as she put it on. This would be the first time she would wear a swimsuit and go to the beach with a guy. Trying to calm her nerves, she pulled her hair back into a ponytail, threw on a shirt and shorts over the suit, and slipped her feet in sandals.

When she finished, Sammie was already standing by the door. His T-shirt fit tighter than his usual shirts, showing his slim but muscular frame.

Realizing she was standing there gawking, River hurried to put distance between him and her wayward thoughts. Sammie gave her a nice distraction from having to forgive her parents. She had to stop letting them ruin her life.

As he drove toward the beach, River's thoughts kept returning to the things her parents had done. No matter how she tried to let those thoughts go, they kept bombarding her brain. Letting balloons go, popping them, or releasing a big fish would be much easier than forgiving someone who didn't deserve forgiveness.

Holding onto hurt and anger wasn't causing her parents any discomfort. Not forgiving them wasn't making their lives unhappy, but it sure was making her miserable.

She'd been so wrapped up in her anger for so long; how could she ever let go?

Chapter 19

A gentle breeze offset the warm sun as River wiggled her toes into the sand and watched the gentle ocean waves. Although the beach was busy with people swimming and sunbathing, Sammie had found a semi-secluded spot by the sand dunes. She was surprised he not only had brought a blanket but two towels.

He'd driven them through a fast food place, they'd eaten hamburgers in his pickup, and now they sat together on the beach. Content in the silence, River watched seagulls gliding in the salty breeze.

"Are you feeling better?" Sammie gave her a concerned look.

Just being with him helped. "Yeah, I am. Thank you. I probably should have eaten breakfast before church."

Sammie chuckled. "So, you are one of those hangry people?"

"Hangry?"

"Yep, when hungry, you get angry. One of my brothers is like that. He is easygoing and nice until he gets hungry. Then, you better watch out because he gets meaner than a mad dog."

River grinned. "So, it's not just me?"

Sammie looked serious. "You are not alone in your struggle. And now that I know, I will always keep a protein or candy bar handy when we go anywhere."

She tried to stay serious but couldn't help but grin. "That probably would be much safer."

Sammie stood and offered his hand. "Want to go swimming?"

River glanced at the ocean. The waves didn't look too big, and even little kids were playing in the surf. Maybe it would be okay. She placed her hand in his and rose to her feet.

He wove his fingers into hers and led her into the water. She gasped as the cool water rose to her knees. Sammie continued guiding her deeper into the ocean until they were past the breaking waves. Even though her feet could still touch the sandy bottom, the movement of the water up to her chest made her nervous.

Sammie squeezed her hand. "Don't be afraid. I've got you."

"But who has you?"

"Good point." Sammie chuckled. "Would you feel more comfortable closer to shore?"

"Yes, please."

His grin turned mischievous as he tightened his grip on her fingers. "Get ready to run."

"No, wait." As much as River could, she planted her feet. "What are you talking about?"

"You've never done the surf run?"

"I have never heard of anything like that."

Sammie got that serious look again. He tsked. "Such a shame. You have missed so much in your young life. It's a Banks family special." Before she could react, he took off running and pulling her through the surf.

Squealing and laughing, she tried to keep up with his fast pace as they ran through the waves.

When they returned to their blanket, River collapsed. "That was so much fun."

"I know, right? Want to do it again?"

She stifled another squeal. "Yes!"

For the next few hours, they ran and played in the surf as Sammie showed her all sorts of goofy, enjoyable games to play in the water. She'd never had so much fun in her life.

Happily exhausted, River sat next to Sammie on the blanket. Drawing her legs against her chest, she locked her arms around them.

Sammie, lying on his back, had his eyes closed. From his rhythmic breathing, he must have been asleep. River sighed. What a perfect day.

The sound of laughter drew her attention. A little girl, with her hands held by her mother and father, played in the water.

The familiar ache twisted in River's chest. Why couldn't she have had a loving family like that? Why didn't her parents love her? Why didn't she have fun memories like Sammie had with his family? It wasn't fair. How could she ever forgive her parents?

River shoved to her feet as she tried to stop the tears. Sammie must have been asleep because he didn't move. She walked to the water and kept going until it was up to her chest.

In front of her, the ocean stretched for miles and miles. All her bad memories were like hooks, drawing her deeper into anger and depression. How could she ever get free?

Forgive.

The word came inside her but around her, a voice offering freedom. She knew the sacrifice of Jesus Christ washed away sin, but how could forgiving her parents bring her freedom? It didn't make sense. They didn't deserve forgiveness.

A wave struck and knocked her over. River struggled to regain her footing as another wave hit.

A strong hand grabbed hers and pulled her up and forward. Her head broke free of the water. She sputtered and gasped for air.

Sammie had her. He helped her to shallower water, pulled her against his chest, and held her tight. "It's okay. Take a deep breath. I've got you."

A sob ballooned out of her throat, and she clung to him as all the anger and hurt broke free. She didn't know how long they stood together in the water, but she let her tears flow as she silently prayed.

God, I want to be forgiven. Forgive me, please, and please help me forgive my parents. I can't do this on my own. Jesus, if you asked us to forgive others like you have forgiven us, I need your help. I want to let it all go. Lord, I forgive them. Please forgive me, too.

Sammie held River as she cried. How he wished he could take away her pain and fix whatever happened. He prayed for her, for God's comfort, and for wisdom regarding what he should do.

He held her close but not too tight. He'd stand and hold her as long as River let him. And someday, maybe, God would let him hold her as more than just a friend.

Chapter 20

Embarrassed by her meltdown, River stepped out of Sammie's embrace and wiped her eyes. "I'm sorry. I shouldn't have cried."

Sammie reached for River, gently pulled her back into his arms, and held her against his chest. "You don't need to ever apologize for your emotions. Crying is cleansing. Even guys cry."

"Really?"

"Really." His eyes tender, Sammie gazed down at her. "It might not be the macho thing to do, but yeah, when life hurts, our bodies react." His chest puffed out. "Even manly men like me have been known to leak some tears."

River returned the grin of her handsome friend. In the gentle rocking motion of the water, she stayed in Sammie's arms. Between running, playing in the surf, and crying, her legs barely could hold her up.

She couldn't believe she'd actually forgiven her parents. Her past hadn't changed, but she felt like she finally had a future. She'd never felt so relaxed and free.

"Get a room!" A group of teenage guys laughing and hooting swam past them.

Sammie cleared his throat, took River's hand, led her back to their blanket, and handed her a towel. "Sorry about that. I hope you don't mind me holding you."

Even though her skin was warm from being in the sun most of the day, her cheeks heated. "I don't mind at all."

His grin flipped toward her as he dried off. "Good to know."

Grateful she had a towel in her hand, River stayed busy getting water and sand off instead of jumping into Sammie's arms. It wasn't like they were dating or anything serious, but she sure wouldn't mind if they were. If they did start dating, maybe she could get lots more hugs and kisses.

Sammie rolled up his towel. "Since it's getting late, I better get you something to eat before you get hangry."

"Now that you mention food, I am hungry, but after being outside all afternoon, I don't think a restaurant would want me inside."

"No problem. I can drive us through somewhere. But next time, I'll take you somewhere nice."

"Next time?"

"That is if you would like to keep dating."

"Dating? We're dating?" River's voice squeaked, and a nervous laugh slipped out.

Sammie nodded, his expression hopeful. "I'd like to date you if that would be okay."

"Yes, I'd love to." River bounced on her toes. She couldn't believe it. Sammie wanted to date her! She was really dating someone.

"Well, okay. It's official."

"Really? It is? We're officially dating? So, what do we do now? Are we supposed to kiss or something to make it more official." At least she was hopeful that was the tradition.

"Now, that's an excellent idea." Sammie's kiss made her heart sigh.

He stepped back. "There. We're officially sealed with a kiss."

"I'm excited. Thank you. I've never dated anyone before."

Sammie's head tilted. "You haven't?"

River swallowed hard. Maybe she shouldn't have admitted that fact. Would Sammie think something was wrong with her? "I mean. I just never had an opportunity because of school and taking care of Nana. I like guys, but I had to always be at the house and uh, well..." River closed her mouth. She was making things worse. Ugh. She shouldn't have said anything.

"Hey." Sammie put his hand under her chin and tilted her head up to look at him. "I'm grateful to be your first official dater. River, I haven't dated that much either, so we'll take it slow and enjoy being together."

"I'd like that. Very much."

"Me too. Let's get you something to eat and get you home. Monday morning will be here before we know it."

That night, River lay in bed and stared at the ceiling. Today had been the perfect day. She was officially dating Sammie Banks and tomorrow Faith was taking her to get her driver's license.

River grinned. She would soon be an official South Carolina Crawdad Beach resident. But before she went to the DMV, she needed to get the documents ready.

Rising out of bed, she crossed to her closet to check inside her suitcases. Before she'd left Texas, Nana had given River an envelope, telling her it would give her the information she needed for the next part of the journey. Hopefully, she'd find her social security card and birth certificate.

Where was it? River searched through her suitcases, looking through them both, but she still couldn't find the information. She tried again. Reaching deep into a side pocket, River's fingers touched something that felt like a large envelope. Yes! Maybe this would have what she needed.

She emptied the contents on her bed and found her birth certificate and social security card. There was even another envelope with her name written in Nana's handwriting on the front.

Her grandmother had left her a letter? How sweet. River couldn't wait to see what it said. Stretching out on the bed, she opened the envelope and held the paper.

As she read the words, River's vision blurred and swam. Why hadn't they told her?

Nana's letter explained no one knew who River's father was, but her birth mother had been a pregnant, drugged-up teenager who died in childbirth. If that wasn't bad enough, River's birth mother was Nana's daughter, which meant her adopted dad was her uncle and Nana really was her blood relative. River's stomach churned. She had been adopted, and they were all family. Why hadn't they told her?

Her grandmother admitted in the letter if she had known what would happen, she would have let River be adopted by someone else. Nana also explained that when she had her accident, she agreed to give River's "parents" all her money and house as long as River stayed safe. That's why her grandmother had told her to leave if anything happened to her and never return. Her so-called parents had planned on kicking River out when she graduated from high school.

River curled into a ball, put a pillow over her face, and screamed.

Chapter 21

She should have called in sick. Silent sobs shook River's shoulders as she clung to the restaurant bathroom sink. She looked up at the ceiling and kept her voice quiet. "Show me where You were, God. Please show me the good. Show me something good from when I lived with my parents. I've forgiven them, but knowing what I know now makes it even worse. It hurts so much."

At a knock on the door, she straightened and scrubbed her face. "I'll be out in a minute." River checked her reflection in the mirror and groaned. It was apparent she'd been crying.

"Are you okay?" Faith Hollis's sweet voice came from the other side of the door.

"I'm fine. Thank you." River tried to keep her voice light. "I'll be out in a minute." Crawdad Beach had given her a safe place to live, but it didn't mean the past still didn't hurt.

Hurrying to resume her waitress duties, she shoved her hair behind her ears, took a deep breath, plastered on a smile, and returned to work.

Faith came beside her. "Sweet girl, are you sure you're okay?"

"Of course." River smiled her best. "Thank you for checking."

Faith nodded, but her eyes still showed concern. "Let me know if you need anything, okay?"

"I will. Thank you." She felt bad that she had caused Faith to worry, but how could River explain what she was feeling?

As she waited on tables, the ache intensified in her chest. Happy families were throughout the restaurant. Eric and Crystal were at a table with her daughter, Olivia, and her husband, Marcus. Grace and her husband, Jeremy, sat with his Aunt Helen. Wilder, Stella, David, and Marie, with their twins, were with Henry Doss. Everyone had a family but her.

She was dating Sammie, but how long would that last? Even when she was a baby, she hadn't been wanted.

Trying to keep herself together, River picked up the plates for one of her tables and returned to the kitchen.

"Hi, friends." Maybelline carried a big sack into the room. "We brought fresh peaches we bought at the orchard."

"Wonderful! Thank you," Faith said. "I can't wait to make a cobbler with them."

"River, how are you doing?" Maybelline asked. "I've heard great things about you working here."

"She's doing a wonderful job," Faith beamed at River.

"Thank you, both." At least something was going right.

"Hey," Ursula almost bumped into River. "Sammie was in, but he just left."

"He left? Why?"

"Not sure. He said something about needing to get back to the store."

River bit her lip to keep it from trembling. Did he not want to talk to her? Was Sammie going to get rid of her, too? She didn't think she could handle anything else.

"Don't forget," Faith called from the stove area. "we'll leave soon to get your driver's license. We can drop by your place if you want to change out of your work clothes."

River nodded. "Thank you." She needed to focus, do her job, get her license, and maybe after work, she could find out why Sammie had left.

But what if he changed his mind and no longer wanted to date her? *Oh, God.* She prayed for help because she didn't think she could take one more heartache.

That afternoon, her new driver's license tucked in her purse, River sat in Faith's car as she drove them back to Crawdad Beach. The time at the DMV had gone well, and she was grateful she'd been able to wear one of her new outfits, but she still couldn't stop worrying about what she'd found out in the letter. Why couldn't she have had a sweet woman for a mom like Faith, Maybelline, or Lila's mother?

"Do you want to tell me what's been worrying you?" Faith glanced her way, then returned her gaze to the road.

River readjusted in her seat. Should she say anything? She'd hate for Faith to think badly of her.

"I'm not asking as your employer," Faith said. "I'm asking as a friend. I'd like to help in any way I can."

"I found out some things about my birth that I didn't know."

Faith gave her a curious glance. "Do you want me to pull over so we can talk?"

"No, please keep driving. It will be easier to tell you without you looking at me. After the sermon about our thoughts and forgiving others, I knew I needed to forgive my parents, and I did it, which was helpful. I did feel better, but then I found a letter from my Nana explaining about my birth."

"Your birth?"

River took a deep breath and shared what she'd discovered, how she was raised, and what she went through as a kid.

Faith's eyes were watery when she glanced her way. "Oh, sweet girl. I'm so sorry."

River swiped the tears running down her cheeks. "I forgave my parents before I found out the rest of my story. But now, I feel even worse. Since we're all related, I don't understand why they didn't want me. My grandmother was good to me, but my parents, I mean my aunt and uncle, treated me like their personal slave. I've been praying that God would help me remember something positive about my childhood. Because I'm wondering if God was even with me."

"God was, and is, with you. He brought you to Crawdad Beach, didn't He?"

River scoffed. "Only because my car blew up."

"True, but I believe God directed you to us. He does that for His children even when we don't see Him or know He is with us. River, would you still forgive your parents even if you can't think of anything good?"

She sucked in a breath. "I already forgave them, but do I need to keep doing it? That would stink."

"I know it's not easy. The past can't be changed, but you can choose whether your hardships make you better or bitter. Resentment and bitterness are poisons that only poison yourself. Remember, forgiving others doesn't free them; it frees you."

River shook her head. "You don't know all the rotten things my parents did."

"You're right. I don't know all you've been through." Faith stayed quiet for a little while. "Would it be okay if I shared a little of my story?"

River shrugged. "Sure."

Faith kept her eyes on the road as she continued driving. "I graduated high school early and came to Crawdad Beach as a seventeen-year-old runaway. I left home with only a bag of clothes and thirty-four dollars in my pocket. My parents were drug addicts who beat me, and the only time I had heard the name of Jesus was when they used His name as a curse word.

"Tiddlywinks hired me as a waitress, and one of the town's widows, Dora, let me stay in her spare bedroom. My rent was provided by helping Dora around her house and yard. Dora showed me love I'd never known, became like my second mom, and taught me the truth about Jesus. When I accepted Christ as Savior, Dora changed my real name to Faith. A year later, I married George Hollis, whose family owned Tiddlywinks.

"God blessed me with Jesus as my Savior and then later with George as my husband. My life drastically changed, but my past remains. Looking back at all the bad memories doesn't help me or anyone else. Now, when I think back, all I need to do is praise God that I was rescued from that situation and given a new life."

River sat still, trying to process. "That explains why you and everyone else were so nice when I came to town."

Faith nodded. "River, everyone has a story. You'd be surprised to learn what most people who live in Crawdad Beach have lived through."

"But I don't know how to do the forgive and forget thing."

Faith reached over and gave River's arm a gentle pat. "Forgiving doesn't mean the past is erased. Many difficult memories will fade away in the light of God's grace, but some will remain. It's okay to grieve over what you experienced and what was lost, but don't get stuck there.

God gives new days with His new mercies. Bring your past into God's light and truth and release it into His loving hands. With every step of obedience in forgiving others gives another step in your freedom."

Chapter 22

A dove cooed in the tree branches above as River sat watching the water sparkle in the late afternoon sunshine. She had explained to Faith that she needed time alone, so once they returned to Crawdad Beach, she'd dropped River at the town park.

The faint fragrance of flowers surrounded her, and in front of her, the water flowed free. Why couldn't she be free? Did she have to keep forgiving her parents? River groaned.

How did Faith let her past go? Why did Jesus say to forgive, and then we would be forgiven? It wasn't fair. River crossed her arms over her chest. Her parents didn't deserve forgiveness.

River's stomach clenched as the realization hit her: she didn't deserve forgiveness either. Nothing she had done, or ever could do, would be good enough to stand before a holy, perfect God.

River put her head in her hands. "God, I thought I had forgiven them. But after Nana's letter, I feel like I did before. I can't do this on my own. Please help me. I don't want the past to keep messing with me. Please help me."

As she sat praying, memories ran through her mind. Getting angry, she got to her feet and stomped down the trail.

Would she ever be able to think about her past without getting mad? A crow screeched in the distance. She wanted to screech, too. Why wasn't there a magic button where she could erase the bad memories?

River blew out a breath. She had to stop replaying everything negative because it sure wasn't helping her peace of mind. And it wasn't doing anything to change what happened.

A slight movement in the bushes ahead drew her attention. Taking quiet steps, River crept forward. A little rabbit was stuck in a thorny vine.

"Oh, no. Poor baby." She knelt next to the bunny, and it jerked back, trying to escape. "It's okay. I'll help."

Praying the little thing wouldn't be so scared, River put her hands on its back. The rabbit stilled. "That's right. I'm going to get you free." River gently worked the vine away from the bunny's back feet and let it go.

The bunny ran a few feet away, stopped, then turned around as though thanking her and hopped away.

Tears streaming down her face, she looked up at the sky. "You want me to be free too, don't You? Okay, God, I forgive my family. And please help me to stop getting my thoughts tangled in the thorns of my past."

River went off the trail and walked along the sandy riverbank. With each step she took, she imagined she was leaving behind her past.

A memory returned of the kind school bus driver whose wife would prepare lunches for River that included encouraging notes, and every day, the couple would walk her home and make sure she was safe. The faces of numerous schoolteachers came to mind who took a special interest in helping her with homework.

When River was left alone on weekends, Lila and her parents would come to get her, take her to their house, and bring her back before her parents knew she had been gone.

Then, when Nana had her accident and came to live with them, she stayed in the River's room, giving her friendship and comfort and keeping her safe from her parent's wild parties. The best part was that Nana introduced River to Jesus Christ.

River stopped. Although her life had been difficult, she'd never been out of God's care.

Chapter 23

A few minutes before Tiddlywinks was set to close, Sammie pushed open the restaurant door and looked around. He didn't see River. Had she already gone home?

Ursula stepped around the corner. "Hi, Sammie. We're about to close."

"Yeah, I know. I was looking for River."

"Faith took her to get her driver's license, so she won't be coming back here this evening."

"Oh, okay. Thanks." Sammie left, crossed the street, and walked to River's house. Once he arrived, he sat on her concrete porch and leaned against her door. He'd wait until she came home.

"Sammie?"

Lost in a dream, he heard River's voice calling him. He grinned at the sweet sound.

"Sammie."

Someone was patting his arm.

"Sammie. Wake up."

He jolted and found River staring down at him. "Hi."

"Hey." Sammie got to his feet and wiped off his jeans. "What are you doing here?"

River grinned. "I live here."

He looked around and finally realized where he was. "That's right. I was worried about you. Is everything okay?"

"It's much better now." River unlocked her door and stepped inside. "I got my driver's license today." She slipped off her shoes, sat on the couch, and gazed at him as he sat in the chair across from her. "I heard you came to the restaurant this morning. Why did you leave before I got to see you?"

"I thought you were upset with me."

"No, it's not you. You're great. I found out something last night. My grandmother left me a note explaining about my adoption."

"You were adopted?"

River's shoulders drew up. "Yeah, I knew that but didn't know anything about my birth."

Sammie moved to the couch and sat next to her. "You want to talk about it?"

"It's complicated, and I don't want you to think I'm weird."

"You're not weird. I wouldn't think that."

"You might." River looked away.

"No way. I think you're great. You're beautiful and fun to be with and talk to."

"Promise me, you'll still like me if I tell you."

He crossed his heart. "I promise."

River took a deep breath and started talking. She told him in an almost monotone voice about her adoption, her family, how she grew up, and how and why she left Texas and got to Crawdad Beach. It was as though she was telling someone else's story. "And that's my messed up life."

He couldn't believe all she'd gone through and couldn't imagine. "I'm sorry, River. I wish things had been different for you. But you sure did turn out great."

She tilted her head as she looked at him. "You think so?"

"I know so. Look at you. You were born to a teenager with a drug problem and adopted by your aunt and uncle, who didn't seem to even want you. You took care of them, your grandmother, and you. You graduated high school. And all by yourself, even though you barely had any money, didn't know where you were going, had a car blow up on you, you made it to Crawdad Beach, have a job, a nice place to live, and people who care about you."

River blinked a few times, and a shy smile crossed her lips. "I like your version much better."

"It's your story. From what you told me, it was tough, but you made it to the other side. River, it's just not what you've been through but who you have become. You are amazing, and I'm very grateful God helped you through all those cruddy times."

Sammie pulled her to her feet and wrapped her in a hug. Wishing he could take away her pain, he held her close and kissed the top of her head. "I can't change the past for you, but I sure would like to be in your future."

"I'd like that very much."

Chapter 24

"Will you be going to Tiddlywinks this evening?" Gloria gave Sammie a knowing grin.

He grinned right back at her. "You know it. Are you coming, too?"

"Yes, I wouldn't miss it for the world."

Eric walked toward the door. "I'll run by the bakery and meet you both there."

"I'll take care of locking up," Gloria said.

Sammie checked his watch. He needed to hurry and finish everything so he could get there on time. He and River had been officially dating for seven months and seven days. It was a perfect number, and if all went well by seven o'clock tonight, the day would end on a perfect note.

The store door opened, and Chester peeked inside. "You all need to hurry. River's friend, Lila, is already here. She's hanging out at Knick Knacks with Jeremy and Grace until time. The restaurant is packed. I think everyone in town is there. Do you need me to do anything else?"

"I think everything is ready," Sammie said.

Gloria laid her hand on Sammie's arm. "Are *you* ready?"

He took a deep breath. "Ready as I'll ever be."

She hugged him. "I'm so proud of you." When she stepped back, her eyes were moist.

"Thanks, second Mom." He chuckled but was having trouble not getting a little misty-eyed himself.

"Now, get going." Gloria gave him a gentle shove.

Sammie checked his pocket to make sure the velvet box was still inside. Thank goodness Chester had a friend in the jewelry business. Sammie just hoped what he bought would be something River would always be proud to wear.

River couldn't believe how crowded the restaurant was this evening; they even had a line out the door. It was strange how everyone on staff was working like crazy but still in a great mood. Maybe because it was Friday?

Either way, people were happy and tipping well. What was strange is they didn't leave; they just sat around and kept talking. Maybe it was a special day for the town or something. She had to admit it was fun seeing so many people she knew.

Her life had changed in wonderful ways since she came to Crawdad Beach. She and Sammie had been dating for seven months, and his family had welcomed her with open arms.

"River!" Faith called to her from the back. "Could you help me for a moment?"

River hurried to follow Faith to her office.

Faith rummaged around in one of her file cabinet drawers. "I know it's in here somewhere."

"How can I help?"

"Just a minute, let me see if I can find it."

Confused, River stood by Faith's desk. Why was she called to find something if she couldn't help look?

Faith hummed as she continued to flip through files. "Just a few more minutes. Why don't you take a seat and rest while I continue to look."

Didn't she need to get back to work? River sat and stared at Faith as she hummed away.

Faith's head popped up, and she smiled her way. "Do you have the time?"

River checked the clock on the wall. "It's two minutes until seven."

"Good. Okay. Let's stop by the kitchen for a minute and then get back on the floor."

"Didn't you need me to find something?"

"Oh, that." Faith waved her hand. "No worries. It's all taken care of now."

River followed Faith to the kitchen, but no one was there. Where was everyone?

Faith didn't seem the least bit concerned. "I guess it's time. Come on."

What on earth was going on? River had to rush to keep up with Faith's hurried pace.

The place was still full, but everyone was just sitting there smiling.

"River."

At Sammie's voice, she turned.

He walked toward her and took her hand. "River Sawyer, you are the most amazing woman I have ever met. I'm grateful God brought you to our town. I love you. I'm not the richest or strongest guy, but I promise to love, care, and provide for you." He got down on one knee and held out a black velvet box with a beautiful diamond ring. "Would you do me the honor of marrying me?"

A happy sob tore through her throat. "Yes!"

Applause erupted from the room as streamers were thrown into the air.

Sammie hugged her close. "I'm so glad you said yes because if not, this would have been the most embarrassing day ever. I love you, River Sawyer."

"I love you too, Sammie Banks."

"Just think," Chester yelled, "your name will be River Banks. If you have a son, you can name him Rich Banks, and a daughter could be Penny Banks. Just don't name her Piggy."

"You are not helping," Sammie playfully growled as he placed the ring on River's finger.

A squeal came from behind her, and she was enveloped in a hug. Turning, she found herself in Lila's arms.

"I'm so happy for you!" Her friend squeezed her tight.

River giggled. "I can't believe you're here."

"I wouldn't miss this for the world. Sammie and I have been in touch. Mom and Dad send their love and will be here for the wedding. And I'm staying for a few days to help buy you a dress with my Mom's credit card. They always considered you their other daughter. Plus, you're their favorite. And Dad asked if you would let him give you away at the wedding."

River sucked in a sob. "Oh, that's so sweet. I would be honored to have him walk me down the aisle." She looked at the ring sparkling on her finger. "I can't believe I'm going to be married."

Sammie cleared his throat. "Could I cut in, please?"

Wrapped tight in his arms, River gave him a kiss she hoped would forever seal the deal.

Epilogue

In the crisp, clean morning air, River sat next to Sammie on the deck of their honeymoon cabin overlooking a valley in the Blue Ridge Mountains.

She smiled at the memory of Faith, Maybelline, Ursula, Sammie's mom, Lila, and Lila's mother hovering around River as they worked on her hair and makeup before the wedding. She would never forget the precious moments of Lila's dad walking her down the aisle and seeing Sammie dressed in a tux waiting for her. She couldn't believe she was actually married to Sammie.

"Mrs. Banks." Her sweet husband grinned at her. "Would you like to go on a hike? Or, we could go back inside and, um, spend some more time together." He shimmied his eyebrows.

River giggled. "I *love* spending time with you."

He chuckled. "Oh, man, I *love* spending time with you too." Grabbing her hands, he pulled her to her feet and wrapped her in a hug. "Did you know I've been praying for you as long as I can remember?"

"You have been?"

"Yep. My parents and I prayed for the woman I was supposed to marry. Since I'm a few years older than you, that means you've been surrounded by our prayers all your life. And to be honest, I had no idea God would bless me with anyone as wonderful as you."

River sighed as Sammie held her close. Closing her eyes, she whispered to God a prayer of thanks.

To the Reader

Thank you for taking the time to read *River Steps Free*. When I began River's story, I didn't know much about her past other than she was desperate to remember something good from her childhood.

Perhaps you can identify with my character and her difficulties. I understand. Life is hard, and people can be cruel.

Throughout the historical accounts in the Bible, people were persecuted, put in horrible situations, taken from loving families, abused, and mistreated. Yet, we can read about their positive ending and how God turned what the enemy meant for evil into good.

Your story isn't over. Whatever you've gone through, whatever you are going through, or whatever you might go through in the future, Jesus knows how you feel. He was (and is) perfect and sinless. During His time on earth, He went around doing good, healing people, feeding thousands, and preaching the good news, yet Jesus was hated, persecuted, falsely accused, beaten, and crucified. He rose again, and His tender heart beats in love. Jesus knows how you feel.

What you were in the past, whatever was done to you, whatever you did, Jesus washes clean and restores what the enemy has stolen.

God is a healing, redeeming, comforting God. He heals the brokenhearted and binds their wounds. God's grace and mercy forgives our sins. In the same way, we must forgive others, and in return, we are forgiven and set free.

Like River, let's step into God's freedom.

Heavenly Father, thank You for Your forgiveness and for helping us forgive others. Shine Your light on the dark areas of our past with Your truth, healing, and restoration.

"To forgive is to set a prisoner free and discover that the prisoner was you." ~ Lewis B. Smedes

"For if you forgive people their wrongdoing, your heavenly Father will forgive you as well. But if you don't forgive people, your Father will not forgive your wrongdoing." (Matthew 6:14-15, HCSB)

"Do not remember the past events, pay no attention to things of old. Look, I am about to do something new; even now it is coming. Do you not see it? Indeed, I will make a way in the wilderness, rivers in the desert." (Isaiah 43:18-20, HCSB)

Acknowledgments

Heavenly Father, thank You for the amazing blessing of Your grace, forgiveness, and mercy. Thank You for the stories You bless me to write. I can never repay You for Your kindness and love.

To my sweet husband, Dennis, thank you for your love and friendship and for being a wonderful husband. I'm so grateful the Lord brought us together.

Patricia (PacJac) Carroll, thank you for your friendship, edits, suggestions, and the fun you bring to the writing journey.

Jack Foster, thank you again for your creative Crawdad drawings used throughout the Crawdad Beach Series. Readers, please visit Jack at jackfosterart.com

Readers, thank you for taking the time to read my book. If you liked the novel, would you be so kind as to leave a positive review and tell your friends about the book? Thank you!

About the Author

Lisa Buffaloe is a happily married mom, multi-published author, and speaker. She enjoys spending time with God, Bible study, writing, hanging out with her sweet husband, and God's beautiful nature.

Please visit Lisa at https://lisabuffaloe.com

Books by Lisa

Fiction

Crawdad Beach Series
Visible, yet Hidden
Running to Grace
Crystal's Journey Home
A Baker's Heart
Stella's Heart Code
River Steps Free

Hope and Grace Series
Nadia's Hope
Prodigal Nights
Writing Her Heart
The Discovery Chapter
Open Lens

The Masterpiece Beneath
The Fortune
Grace for the Char-Baked

Non-Fiction
Float by Faith
Heart and Soul Medication
Time with The Timeless One
The Forgotten Resting Place
Present in His Presence
We Were Meant for Paradise

One Lit Step: Devotions for your journey
The Unnamed Devotional
Flying on His Wings
Unfailing Treasures
No Wound Too Deep For The Deep Love of Christ
Living Joyfully Free Devotional (Volumes 1 & 2)

Thank you for reading,

River Steps Free

Lisa Buffaloe

www.ingramcontent.com/pod-product-compliance
Lightning Source LLC
Chambersburg PA
CBHW071521170626
46811CB00007B/2919